The Scorpion, the code name Madison had been given years ago on a warm, dark Venezuelan night, was coming alive in her again. The code name she had earned that night when a band of extremists had held the Ambassador and three agents of the CIA hostage. The Scorpion, the creature that suddenly moves in on its victim and terminates silently with a venomous sting, had been born on that black night. And tonight, as she slipped the ski mask over her head and trotted noiselessly down the beach, she welcomed back that part of herself. Her mind focused on one thing only: freeing Terry at any price.

From her spot on the beach, the house looked like a great, huge, shadowy box, sitting alone above the water without a neighbor within a half mile, one dim light glowing in the living room.

How many patrols were waiting? How many nameless faces between her and Terry?

# A SINGULAR SPY

*A Madison McGuire Espionage Thriller*

## AMANDA KYLE WILLIAMS

The Naiad Press, Inc.
1992

Printed in the United States of America on acid-free paper
First Edition

Edited by Katherine V. Forrest
Cover design by Pat Tong and Bonnie Liss
   (Phoenix Graphics)
Typeset by Sandi Stancil


**Library of Congress Cataloging-in-Publication Data**

Williams, Amanda Kyle, 1957–
   A singular spy / by Amanda Kyle Williams.
      p.      cm.
   ISBN 1-56280-008-6
   I. Title.
PS3573.I447425S5    1992
813'.54--dc20                                              91-38259
                                                              CIP

## About the Author

Amanda Kyle Williams was born in August of 1957 and spent her formative years near Boulder, Colorado. At the age of sixteen, she left high school for a full-time job. By the age of twenty-eight, she was vice-president of a sizeable textile manufacturing company.

At thirty, she walked away from corporate America and began work on the first espionage-action thriller to feature a lesbian agent. She now resides in Marietta, Georgia with her partner Julie and their ever-growing family of cats.

Amanda Kyle Williams is also the author of *Club Twelve* and *The Providence File*.

*For Julie, of course.*

# Prologue

A cold and cloudless evening. A simple brush pass on a bright, snow-capped Geneva night. Information for cash, information or blackmail ... As had been done so many times before, in so many cities with so many buyers, so many sellers.

But for Lyle Dresser the exchange about to take place was anything but routine. He had locked up his embassy office on this night as he had on hundreds of nights before, gone to his favorite restaurant as he always did to delay going home to his wife, and eaten his usual sausage sandwich and

1

drank warm lemon vodka for courage. But tonight the sausage felt like granite in his stomach and his plump hands had trembled as he brought the glass mug to his lips.

*Do everything as you normally would,* they had told him. *Do not alter your routine an iota.*

And they, whoever *they* were, for he did not know and did not want to know, had guaranteed him that if he refused to cooperate, the proof of his indiscretions with the embassy secretary would be delivered to his wife.

Lyle Dresser had first reacted with bitter disbelief to the threats. "You have no proof. This is an outrage," he had shouted to the male-female team who had intercepted his automobile on a quiet mountain road last Saturday afternoon.

But the woman had patiently laid the photographs in front of him and he had seen himself in young Sasha's arms, seen the silliness of an aging fat man desperately grasping at the passion of his youth.

"A simple list is all we ask from you, Mr. Dresser", the shadowy faces had told him. "A list of Intelligence agents working under diplomatic cover ... A list for your marriage".

"But I am just a clerk," he had told them helplessly.

"A CIA clerk with access to secret files", was the reply.

Now Lyle Dresser took one despondent step after another on the sidewalk slush. "Walk as you normally would, not slower, not faster," they had warned him. "You are a faithful husband going home to your faithful wife."

2

But the despair that had seized Lyle Dresser in the last week would not allow him to accept their soothing words. I am a spy and a traitor, he reminded himself. Faithful to no one, not even to my country.

The vague outline of a woman was coming closer, the coat tightly belted at the waist and curving over her hips. The woman who had climbed into his car, the woman who had shoved the embarrassing photographs in his face.

When she was so close that Lyle Dresser could hear the frozen snow cracking under her boots, he held the folded list at his side, as he had been instructed, and prayed that he would never again be asked to smuggle information out of the embassy files.

And in that split second when her hand rose at him, when Dresser realized that her concealed spike had pierced his heart, he knew that his unfortunate prayer had been answered.

The angle and strength of the thrust was so perfect that instant paralysis resulted. No air passed through the vocal cavity, no sound was made, no passerby was alerted to the brutal murder.

The executioner never slowed. She was a professional in the art of silent killing, and her gloved hand had removed the Intelligence from the pudgy clerk before he hit the ground.

# — 1 —

The ground descended sharply before her, sinking
into the darkness like headlights on an empty road.
Over the quiet whistle of the wind she heard dogs
barking, chewing up the distance between her and
her pursuers, and then she was running, running
faster than she had ever run in her life. Stumbling,
she felt the rocks bruising her body as she rolled
down the hill, felt twigs and broken tree limbs, felt
her heart pounding against her chest.

The ground evened out abruptly and she found
herself sprawled in a marsh. She lay still for a

moment, listening for the dogs, barely aware of the cold water seeping into her clothing. Just ahead she saw the observation tower springing out of the black ground, rising up into the night like an abandoned lighthouse. Two hundred yards to the border, she thought, two hundred yards to the barbed wire.

The spotlight in the tower switched on abruptly. Quickly she loosened the straps on her heavy backpack, let it drop, and darted across the field, the weight of her wet clothing tugging at her legs, sweat stinging her eyes.

The spotlight passed over her. She raised the 9mm Calico and fired at the tower guard. The spotlight froze.

At the wire she searched frantically for the loose section. They had promised her during the briefing it would be there for her escape — one small section of wire just north of the guard tower large enough for her to slip through.

"Shit, it's not here," she muttered.

The dogs again ... closer, howling hysterically at a fresh scent. She spun around and saw the dark shadows emerging from the marsh, heard their boots pounding the wet earth, heard their shouts, their commands ordering her to freeze ... There was only one way out now.

She switched the 9mm to full automatic and opened fire when the patrol was within a hundred yards. She fired until they advanced no longer, until her ears rang from the deafening gunfire, until tears of pure adrenalin streaked her muddy face. And then she heard the quiet voice, the smooth British accent from behind.

Madison McGuire, emerging from the darkness of

the training center's Clandestine Entry Program, congratulated the young black woman. "Well done, Alex. Only two mistakes. You should have started over the wire as soon as the guards were neutralized. The next patrol is only minutes away. And two, you left your backpack behind intact. That's intelligence we wouldn't want the enemy to find."

From yards away Alexandria Kimble could see the trainers and their dogs filing out of the field. Another night of training had ended. She turned and glared at Madison through the wire fence. "So where the hell was my escape route, Madison? Where was the loose section of wire?"

"Things don't always go according to plan in the field, Alex. You were tested tonight on your ability to improvise." Madison smiled, "You're passing the course, by the way."

Alex Kimble wiped the dirt off her face and lowered herself to the ground with a thud. "Thank God."

"Get cleaned up," Madison said. "I'll buy you a cup of coffee."

They stepped into the main building and went downstairs to the coffee shop. Madison saw Alex's hands trembling when she raised the Styrofoam cup to her mouth.

"I remember my first field assignment," Madison offered quietly. "A brush pass in Bonn. A chance to get my feet wet. I'd practiced it a thousand times, but when I saw the contact coming and I knew this was it, *this* was what I had been training for, my heart started to pump so hard I couldn't hear anything but this incredible roaring in my ears."

Alex seemed to brighten, her brown eyes came to life with a sparkle of anticipation. "So what happened?"

"Training," Madison answered. "I went to automatic. I kept moving and I made the pass, sweaty palms and all. It comes back once you're out there."

Alex leaned forward, resting her chin in her hand. "But what did it *feel* like the first time?"

Madison leaned back and closed her eyes for a moment. "It was a stranger on a dark night, pressing some undisclosed secret into my palm. It was me alone out there in the streets, watching, waiting." She laughed. "It was better than sex."

Alex nodded knowingly, as if Madison had made a perfectly natural comment. "You'll be fine," Madison assured her. "You proved tonight that you're capable of doing whatever's needed."

"Can I ask a personal question, Madison? What was it inside you that made you want to do this?"

*I was barely five years old, and already I was rehearsing to be a spy, listening through walls and peeping through keyholes while my father whispered to my mother in her sick bed about his secret missions. And I, understanding none of it, believed that it must be a wonderful, romantic life because mother always seemed happier and healthier whenever he came home from the field. I last saw my mother's face through a keyhole, Alex. I saw them gathered around her bed in our London house. I saw them raise the sheet. I saw tears drying on my father's cheeks when he stepped into the hall and picked me up and passed me the Intelligence I had already gathered on my own. I was born to it, Alex, just like you were.*

Madison answered only, "My father was with the Company. I learned the life from him."

"Did you ever blow it? Did you ever make a mistake in the field you couldn't take back?"

To her left, Madison saw a chair sliding towards the table. Behind it stood Philip Donleavy, grinning. He was well-built and fit, with powerful forearms. His face was leathery and tan like an old ship's captain. Between his brows were deep vertical ridges that looked like the number eleven. Even when he smiled he had a tragic, uncertain look — the same expression of mothers who have raised families, fathers who have seen their children go to war, heroes who have raised flags in the sand. Philip Donleavy had been a trainer at the "Farm" for six years.

"What, are you kidding?" he asked, straddling the chair. "She almost killed me once."

Alex studied him for a moment, smiling, then looked to Madison for confirmation.

"It was a long time ago," Madison said, with amusement.

"We were in England," Philip began in the voice of a man who liked to remember. "It was her second time out." He turned his powerful body slightly away from Madison as he spoke. "We were posing as weapons buyers out of Dublin, trying to track the supply line on some stuff we thought was going to a terrorist group. So Madison's standing at the window in this little flat while I talked to the seller. All of a sudden, he looks up at her and calls her by her

9

work name. It was something like Constance or Connie."

"Clara," Madison corrected, smiling.

"Right. That was it. Clara," Donleavy resumed. "The guy said it once and then twice and Madison just kept standing there with her back to us. God only knows what she was thinking. So then the paranoid s.o.b. looks at me with these weird, wild eyes and the next thing I know he's behind me with his gun at my head."

Alex had both elbows on the table now, leaning forward, impatiently waiting for Donleavy's next words. She had changed from her dark training clothes into knee-length stretch pants and a short shirt that Madison had seen her wear in the Company gym. She was trim, five-feet-eight inches tall, and when she leaned back, casually crossing an ankle over her knee, Madison saw the long muscles flex in her bare calves.

"Then what?" Alex asked Donleavy.

"Madison whips out her gun." He made his hand into the shape of a gun. "And *boom*. Right there with my head four inches from his. I saw the bullet go right past my nose."

"You can't *see* a bullet, Philip." She looked at Alex. "That was the last time I forgot my work name."

"And that was the last time I went into the field with a green agent," Philip Donleavy added.

Madison smiled. An operation so long past, so many street corners and code names ago, but so clear even now. It had been her coming out as an agent, as so much more. She remembered precisely what she had been thinking about that day, gazing out the window of that tiny flat. Her name was Dorothy. Dorothy who cared for a Company safe house and allowed Madison a glimpse of her through an open bedroom door while she changed — now a bare shoulder, now a nipple, now the curve of her waist. Dorothy who joined Madison in the evenings for "a chat" and carelessly left her robe parted to the top of those magnificent thighs. Dorothy who had changed her life forever . . .

Philip Donleavy's voice interrupted that fond reminiscence. "By the way, the big guy wants to see you as soon as you're done here."

A color-coded badge fastened to her sweater, Madison McGuire walked the seventh floor corridor towards Mitchell Colby's office. Not long ago, she reflected as she stepped through the final check point, she had considered taking a desk job with the agency. It was what Terry wanted more than anything, what Terry had begged her to consider. But after seeing the prison-pale faces that walked the stark corridors of the Central Intelligence Agency, after seeing their strained expressions and their glass cubicles, Madison knew she would not last a month behind agency walls. The field was too much a part of her. It was what she understood, what she had been trained for, what she needed — the unforeseeable twists and turns, the unpredictability, the action.

"Hello, Mr. Colby," she said, entering the large paneled office.

A couch and chairs were arranged in the center,

a long conference table at one end. Unlike the former Director, Madison thought as she looked at the imposing, silver haired figure behind the desk, Colby seemed to need the space. His towering presence filled every inch of the large office. She had often found him sitting on the couch reading, or pacing, or sitting at the conference table staring out the window, lost in his own secret world.

Madison shivered involuntarily. A slight quiver always passed over her behind these walls, a mixture of fear and respect. She had seen Colby and his boys, as he liked to call them — for there were few women in the high ranks of the CIA — sit in this office making plans that would change lives worlds away. Here the guardians of national security gathered, the tacticians and strategists. Individually they were brilliant. Collectively they could be dangerous — absurdly powerful men. And in this room the subject was nearly always power and its open or covert applications.

Now there was a leak in one of the networks. A leak that had already cost the life of a Geneva station clerk. Initially, the CIA had believed that the clerk, Lyle Dresser, had been the sole source of the leak after photographic evidence proved Dresser had removed classified documents from embassy files. But then CIA analysts began sending out bogus Intelligence to each network and peppering the information with special code names for nonexistent operations. Within two weeks the false Intelligence trickled back to Langley from agents-in-place. The analysts and their computers had traced the source of the phony Intelligence to the Swiss networks and it was agreed that Lyle Dresser had only been part of the problem.

Since then, the CIA had been forced to pen escape routes to all but essential personnel in foreign countries, and those few operatives remaining had had their networks slowed to a crawl. Coded radio transmissions had ceased, couriers had stopped carrying, and the CIA was experiencing a sort of paralysis in the vital area of human-generated Intelligence.

"I want you to leave for Geneva as soon as possible," the Director said gruffly to Madison, his grey eyes fixed on her from under bushy white brows. "I've arranged for you to have unrestricted access to the Records Room and to all the personnel files in the Swiss network. Maybe that'll help you trace the leak. Maybe something in the background files will jump out at you. My analysts sure aren't coming up with anything."

Madison thought about that. "This isn't exactly my area, sir. I'll need help from someone who knows the Intelligence markets, who knows what type of buyers buy certain information. If we can track the buyer I think our chances at finding a seller might be increased."

The Director looked tired. His eyes were puffy and red-rimmed. He rubbed his chin and pushed out his thick lips. "We have plenty of qualified analysts available," he said. "Anyone in particular in mind?"

"Donna Sykes," Madison replied, without hesitation.

"Sykes," the Director repeated, writing the name on a note pad. "What's her clearance level?"

Madison pushed away a stray lock of red hair and leaned back in her chair. "She was let go a couple of years ago. Specialized in foreign agents-in-place. One of the best." She paused, her green eyes fixed on the Director. "I wonder if you might consider letting me recruit my own team of specialists for this assignment."

Mitchell Colby studied her for a moment then rambled over to his office window. "So you think we have so many moles in here that we can't run a secure operation?" he asked, after a long silence.

"It just seems prudent to work on the outside until we know what we're dealing with," Madison answered quietly.

The Director returned to his desk. "If we used outsiders we'd have to do it without any official involvement. I couldn't let the Company take the heat if one of your specialists got out of line. We have to retain plausible deniability. You understand what that means, don't you? No protection if there's a problem. No diplomatic help, no deals. Nothing. It's damn tempting, I'll tell you that. God, how I want to nail the sonofabitch selling us out. But it's a risk I can't ask you to take."

"And if I volunteered," Madison responded, searching the old Director's face, "would I still have CIA resources at my disposal? Equipment, records, funds?"

The Director nodded. "We have a certain amount of untraceable funds available to us, yes."

A certain amount, Madison mused, knowing that the CIA had channeled and stored millions in ways Congress — and the President — would never dream possible.

"Oh, there is one other thing, sir," Madison said. "I was scheduled to take out a fresh agent. Her name is Kimble. I'd want her on my team."

"Kimble," he said. "Her mother's assigned to the Washington bureau, FBI, right?"

Madison nodded. "Counter-terrorist division. Alex has talked about her."

Colby shook his head. "I don't know about sending her out in the cold on her first assignment."

"Mr. Colby, Alexandria Kimble is one of the brightest young agents I've seen come out of the center in years. If she's properly trained now, she could make a real contribution later." She paused. "I'm asking as a personal favor, sir. She's counting on me being with her the first time out."

The Director nodded his okay and settled back in his chair, hands folded on his lap. Madison was wearing her operational face, he thought. The face he had seen on so many operatives before a field assignment. They all had their own method of preparation. Some drank and partied and told lies to strangers, some locked themselves up in dark little rooms as if the sunlight might expose their clandestine intent, and others went home, afraid it would be the last time they saw their families. Colby wondered what technique Madison used.

Mitchell Colby's Deputy Directors briefed him every morning at ten promptly. The sessions were relaxed, with coffee and doughnuts on a tray in the center of Colby's conference table, while he and his men plowed their way through stacks of Intelligence reports. Colby always looked over each report, read the summaries and made suggestions where they were needed, for Mitchell Colby was a detail-oriented Director. He involved himself as closely as possible — considering the vast amount of information that crossed his desk and considering that he had not felt well for some time — in the day-to-day operation of the largest Intelligence-gathering agency in the world.

On this morning, however, Mitchell Colby had been preoccupied, had rushed his department heads through the session and quickly dismissed all but Fred Nolan, Deputy Director of Intelligence, William Ryan, Deputy Director of Operations, and Warren Moss, Senior Analyst for Operations.

He opened a thick file bound like a soft cover book and marked: *Operations-Classified Level Two Security.* Moments later he raised his head to address William Ryan.

"I've taken the liberty of stepping into your operations, Will. I'm sending McGuire and Kimble to Geneva. I didn't think you'd have a problem with that."

William Ryan tucked his last bite of doughnut into his cheek and prepared his answer. Ryan was a handsome and boyish fifty, liked by most everyone and very capable of running operations without the Director's help.

"I think Madison's a good choice for Geneva, Mitchell," Ryan answered. "But it *is* customary to consult your head of operations before making operational decisions. That's what you pay me for."

"Point taken," Colby nodded, then quickly moved on. "I want the security level increased on this operation. Only department heads and their analysts are to have clearance. Put it in a black file and be ready to bury it. Madison wants to bring in outsiders."

At this news Fred Nolan raised his balding head. Nolan was fair-skinned, and in his early forties, a bit doughy and rounded on the exterior, but highly intelligent. Professionally he stood out as a man with an eye for detail. Not a great leader in the eyes of the Company, not even a particularly quick learner, but a thorough one indeed. In his personal relationships he was known as devoted but unromantic, had once been overheard expressing the view that marriage was a handicap to be overcome. Yet he had been a faithful husband, and unlike Will Ryan, who had half the Company secretly in love with him, Nolan was not given to even the most innocent of office flirtations.

"This doesn't seem like the kind of operation we'd want outsiders in on, Mitchell," Nolan said carefully. "We can't control them totally and the last thing we need is for news to get out that we have a leak. It's too risky. What's the point?"

Senior analyst Warren Moss saw his opportunity and took it with the kind of enthusiasm that comes easily to the ambitious. "How can we run a secure operation from inside when we have a leak we can't pinpoint? Who in this room would be prepared to guarantee that it doesn't go any deeper than the Swiss networks? If we use a specialty team it keeps the level of inside knowledge to a minimum and we can still monitor them to a point. Seems clear enough to me, Fred."

Fred Nolan and William Ryan exchanged glances.

They hadn't missed it — the stab of disloyalty, the slightest hint at Nolan's lack of foresight, the quickness that marks a fighter from a victim, a climber from a sleeper. Warren Moss had it all. It was business as usual inside the Company.

They often came to this spot after making love, and sat in silence on the deck of the beach house, listening to the waves crash against the brown Carolina coast.

Tonight, Madison thought as their naked bodies huddled together for warmth in their blanket, the moon looked like a London street lamp, cloaked by the moist, yellow fog, its dim light foundering against the darkness.

She wished she could paint. She would paint the sky and the beach as it was tonight, paint Terry as she was tonight, her sweet, dark eyes glistening, her flushed cheeks, her full claret mouth.

She gathered Terry in her arms and squeezed as tightly as she dared, their lovemaking still fresh in her mind, still fresh on her lips.

Tonight Terry had been like a hummingbird in their bed, delicate and weightless and constantly moving, so open and fragile that it had made Madison ache for her, made Madison fear for her.

She loves me too much, needs me too much, she had worried, and then found herself wanting Terry even more, understanding that part of the excitement of love was the uneasiness of knowing the danger.

"How long will you be gone?" Terry asked, so

quietly that Madison scarcely knew she was speaking.

"A few weeks at best," was her reply, and they stayed there for an hour more, holding each other in the cold night air.

# — 2 —

The sign was posted on an old oak tree at the edge of the dirt road and nearly covered by vines. *The Canine Kennel,* it read, and on the front a muscular boxer's head was raised to point visitors in the right direction.

Madison took the narrow, winding road slowly, swerving to miss potholes and trenches, passing clusters of little white homes with aluminum roofs and azalea bushes, then rounding a bend where old willows and young palms crowded the road. Finally the wire of the kennels and the white concrete blocks of the house came into view.

As she got out of the car, she caught a glimpse of a sturdy woman with a water hose and fishing boots up to her knees, washing down the kennel floors while the dogs jumped and barked hysterically in their runs.

If the woman had noticed her at all she gave no indication until Madison was nearly upon her, and then she spoke without turning around. "Help you?"

"I'm looking for Donna Sykes," Madison answered pleasantly.

The woman hosed off her boots, shut off the spigot and brushed her hands off on her jeans. "Have a dog to board?" she asked with a crackling mid-western accent, plunging her big hands into her pockets.

"Actually, no. I'm a friend. We worked together once. Thought I'd pay her a visit."

The woman's brown eyes started at Madison's shoes and slowly moved up over her sweater to Madison's face. "I suppose you're here to ask her a lot of questions like who she talks to and what they talk about." She shook her head and walked back to the spigot. "I told her they'd send a woman next time. Donna chased off the guy that was out a few months back."

Madison smiled and folded her arms over her chest. "Did she now? Well good for her. Those security checks really *are* a bore, aren't they?"

The woman turned, and a slow, wide smile softened the square face. It was a nice smile, Madison thought, seeing the straight row of white teeth and the web of wrinkles that formed around her eyes.

"I'm Pat," she said, returning to shake Madison's hand. "Sorry about the third-degree. But they come creeping around here every few months like they have some claim on Donna or something, upsetting her after they put her out to pasture."

It came from behind Madison — a husky, whooping bellow of a laugh, and then, "I'd know that pair of jeans anywhere. Tell me, Pat, does it speak with a prim little British accent and look like a wildcat?"

Pat chuckled. "Why yes, Don, yes it does."

Madison turned to see tiny Donna Sykes coming towards her, smiling. "Madison McGuire, what brings you out to the boonies?"

"I should ask you the same question," Madison said, looking into Donna's bright little face, the clever blue eyes, the sideways grin that always made you wonder what she was up to.

Donna Sykes threw back her close-cropped silver head and let out a great laugh. "Well, what the hell else would an old dyke do in her retirement?"


The house was spacious, with a view of the bay at the back end. The L-shaped living room was crammed with comfortable furniture, and decorated with paintings and photographs the couple had collected over the years, framed and neatly matted in shades of bluish grey. Madison saw embroidery thread and scissors on one of the end tables, and on the coffee table, a *TV Guide* lying face down, a vase with dried flowers and a clean ashtray. At one end of the room, a well used hammock hung near the glass doors and beyond that a dog was peering inside, waiting for the scraps from dinner.

Outside, a dock stretched fifty feet into the water. On lazy summer days in times past Donna had fished off that old dock, she told Madison, while Pat sunned herself and did her best to keep the dogs quiet and out of the water. They had used the house only as a vacation retreat until Donna's dismissal from the Company two years ago when they packed up and left Virginia. And they hadn't looked back since, Donna said, raising her wine glass. But Donna Sykes had been with the Company for twenty years, and they all knew she had done her share of looking back.

They had dinner at an unfinished pine table off the living room. Pat had found daisies during an emergency visit to the grocery store for an extra steak, and she had arranged them in an old wine bottle at the center of the table.

Madison took a drink of wine and dabbed her mouth with her napkin. "To sum it up, I need someone who can sort through the Intelligence. It'll be coming in on a daily basis, I imagine, and I'll have to be kept up to speed."

Donna Sykes finished her steak and pushed her plate aside. "So the agency gives me the boot. All I get is a hassle every six months and a fruit basket at Christmas. Now you show. What's the catch?"

Madison glanced at Pat then back to Donna. "All I can say right now is that it's an important operation."

Donna sat back in her chair and folded her little

arms across her chest. She watched Madison intently, watched her take another sip from the wine glass, watched her steady hand return the glass to the table, then she smiled and turned to her lover. "Could you leave us for a few minutes?"

Pat stood and laid a hand on Donna's shoulder. "No problem. I've got some cleaning up to do outside."

When the kitchen door closed, Donna grinned cleverly. "Let's have it, McGuire. What's going on?"

"The Geneva station clerk was murdered," Madison answered, taking the napkin from her lap and folding it neatly beside her plate. "We think he was selling secrets, working with someone else who might have become dissatisfied with his performance. Unfortunately that someone is one of ours. The leak is still there. And the catch is, it's not an agency job, not officially anyway."

"So if we get caught running a spy ring in Switzerland our ass is grass," Donna added. "The Swiss are very protective of their neutrality."

Madison reached for a cigarette. "Well, there is a certain amount of risk involved, of course. But I think the security of this country is worth it, don't you?"

How easily the cliches come, Madison thought as the words were leaving her mouth, when you've lived with them all your life, been sworn to them, trained to spread the gospel of the faith.

Donna's blue eyes sparkled. She leaned forward and rested her elbows on the table. "So how the hell did Miss Do-It-By-The-Book get involved in a black operation anyway?"

Madison shrugged. "You make your rules, set

your own schedule. It means working without a safety net, of course, but that's half the fun, isn't it?"

Donna Sykes grinned and clapped her little hands together like a child at the circus. "Oh, you *are* a lunatic, Madison."

When Pat returned from the kennels, Madison joined her in the kitchen. "I hope you're not terribly angry with me for trying to take Donna away like this."

Pat waved one strong hand. "Don's been restless since we've been here and just itching to get into something." She smiled and pointed an accusing finger at Madison. "She's mentioned you before, you know. I didn't remember you at first but I remember the stories now. Did you really use poison darts on a KGB agent?"

Madison could not disguise her astonishment. She glanced at Donna who was sitting at the table smiling. "For the record, Pat, I absolutely do not use Ninja stars, silver bullets or poison darts. Really, Don, you *have* been spinning some tall tales, haven't you?"


There were some complications with the recruitment of the rest of the team. One, living in Dublin, had prior commitments and could not be talked out of them.

Charlie Reach of Glasgow, a failed agent, a former expert in interrogation and a would-be novelist, had to be tracked down and was finally discovered in a Wiesbaden flat, hovering over an old manual typewriter in an alcoholic stupor. Madison walked him, babysat him and fed him chicken soup for a day before she could be sure he was up to the task.

Old George, the photographer, was found in New York City, snapping pictures of babies who did not want to smile by day, and unfaithful spouses by night for a detective agency. Madison could not remember a time when he was called anything but Old George, and she knew no one who remembered there ever being a young George. He had been around the agency on and off for years, working on a contract basis in low to middle level surveillance operations, doing nothing spectacular and never making quite enough money to live on comfortably.

Harley Weatherford, a specialist in electronic penetration, arranged a leave from his own London based private security company and agreed to join the team. Harley's background in Intelligence came from a ten-year stint with the British in research and development. But being an ambitious man with tastes that far exceeded a researcher's salary, Harley Weatherford had left British Intelligence for private enterprise. His company provided telephone and Fax security to corporate accounts; offered high-level, desk-top, and portable scrambling systems; micro-processors that constantly checked telephones for bugs; and advice to executives on a wide array of counter-surveillance measures. Harley was not a field man, had never participated directly in the running of an operation, but he had the wide-ranging expertise in electronics the team would need.

And so, after nearly two weeks, Madison had managed to round up her odd group of specialists for an operation the Company had named Night Trace. They would arrive in Geneva at different times during a three-day period, each carrying one false passport for the trip there, and one Swiss escape passport which had been sown into the lining of his or her suitcase. Each would register in different hotels, and finally they would all meet in the safe house Madison had leased on the edge of the city in the name of the Sovereign Tile Company of Europe.

Oleg Chenlovko locked the door of his meager brown office, removed the middle drawer from his desk and peeled off the tiny camera mounted on the back with a thin strip of velcro. Chenlovko was a Major with the *Komitet Gosudarstvennoi Bezopasnosti's* Second Directorate and one of the few remaining CIA assets left inside the organization. The Major rarely supplied Langley with high level Intelligence but he had been a constant and dependable source of information relating to KGB surveillance operations and basic fieldcraft. But today, he mused as he looked with satisfaction at the document in front of him, had been his lucky day, and all because of the inefficiency of the Soviet courier system. The document delivered from the code room to his desk had been meant for the Colonel upstairs. A document he would normally have never seen.

He had opened the brown envelope knowing the papers within were not for his eyes, but also knowing he could later take the document to the Colonel upstairs and explain the error in delivery.

He would apologize for having opened the envelope by mistake, but after all, it had been delivered to *his* desk.

He spread the papers out and moved all other objects and papers out of the way. He quickly pressed the shutter release several times, removed the film, stuck the camera back in its hiding place and unlocked his office door.

The Americans would be grateful for this information. The Americans, he thought, who held the promise of freedom out like a carrot on a stick. The Americans, who had sent the beautiful Anna to turn him into a spy years ago in a dark bedroom when he was only a security officer. And how she had turned him, so delicately, so carefully, oh so slowly. Don't you want more out of life, Oleg? I know a way. I know people who can help. We must save our country from itself, don't you see?

He often wondered what had become of Anna, wondered how the years had changed her, wondered if she was still linked to the secret Moscow, the Moscow of couriers and informants, of frightened, shadowy figures who move only in the night. She had left him after arranging his first meeting with an American agent. It was no longer safe, she told him. You mustn't have any marks against you. From now on only women with good families and only friends with political connections.

They had waited twelve years for him and they would wait another twelve. They were patient people, the Americans, watching his steady climb and his bright future. One day, perhaps, that future would be reality and his position would carry such merit that they would help him out of Russia, plan his defection, give him a Virginia farm and a pickup truck. But for now, he knew, he was of value only if he stayed in place.

He read over the document excitedly once again. A woman, an intermediary, a free agent of sorts named Natasha Vladov of Czechoslovakia, who apparently supplied the Soviet Union and other countries with Intelligence, had met with a KGB agent in Switzerland. For a substantial amount of money the woman had given the agent the name of a CIA operative working under diplomatic cover in Moscow.

He rode the Metro home that evening then walked to his Leninsky Prospekt address. A vehicle was available to him, sometimes even a driver, but Chenlovko preferred the exercise at least twice a week.

It was a bitter Moscow night. Tears of cold froze on his cheeks. The snow, dirty and brown speckled, was sticking and piling up on the wide streets faster than they could be cleared. Moscow snow was never white for long.

Just ahead he saw a line at a taxi stand. But the taxis weren't stopping tonight. In this weather you don't stop. An old man shivered, half frozen at the rear of the line.

"Walk, old man," Chenlovko told him. "Walk or you'll freeze and the militia will carry you in. No taxis tonight."

His building was square and brown, half of its windows lit with the bluish glow of State-run television. Occasionally one of the tenants hung a makeshift curtain at the windows for privacy, but most Muscovites had long ago given up the idea of trying to hide anything.

He paused at the entrance, and from any distance at all it might have looked like the major was bending to retrieve something from the sidewalk or fastening a bootstrap. But in those few seconds Chenlovko had made a small yellow chalk mark on a certain block near the door. And sometime in the night or the early hours of morning a stranger would pass. By dawn the Americans would know Chenlovko had information. Today, he thought, I work for the Soviet Union, tomorrow against it.

Inside the building, he saw his neighbors' laundry drying on a clothesline on the filthy landing above his flat, the line stretching from their front doorknob to the stairway. He could hear their voices coming from behind the door, shouting. One of his neighbors was always shouting, always fighting, it seemed. But when they heard Chenlovko's boots on the stairs, when they heard his key in the latch, the noise would cease. It was fear that quieted them — one of the benefits of letting your neighbors know you were KGB.

The next morning, his breakfast was a thick slice of black bread warmed in a pan on the burner, and strong coffee — another benefit that came with the job. He had not stood in line for the coffee or for the meat he had eaten the night before. Of course the store where he shopped was not as well-stocked as the Central Committee shops, but there was never a line.

He bought a copy of *Pravda* and walked towards the subway station, his heart pounding with a mixture of fear and exhilaration as it always did before a transfer. He entered the station at the height of the morning rush. Moving with the flow, he joined the cheerless faces waiting for the train, one hand gripping the film canister in the pocket of his greatcoat.

He saw his contact as soon as he boarded, a man he knew only by the work name of Oscar. He moved towards his controller casually, never once making direct eye contact, looking only at the shoes of the people around him. Always look at the shoes, the American had once told him, sometimes the shoes tell you about the person. The clothes may look like you or me, but the shoes have a history.

His controller was sitting near the center of the train and Chenlovko grasped the overhead railing with one hand as the train lurched forward and reached into his pocket for the film with the other, holding it at his side.

In an instant he felt the gloved hand of the American remove the canister. Then, following basic tradecraft, Chenlovko moved on towards the end of the train, distancing himself from the CIA man.

It is done, he thought, done with the graceful motion of one gloved American hand. But what neither Oleg Chenlovko nor his American contact realized was that the man sitting only yards away, dressed in a laborer's coveralls, a battered brown coat and a worn pair of boots, was a KGB officer. And what neither of them could have known was that the KGB officer had been assigned to watch the American, the very American whose name Chenlovko had unwittingly delivered to his Colonel upstairs just yesterday. The same American who was said to be a CIA operative working under diplomatic cover in Moscow.

# — 3 —

The front door opened at eight-fifteen a.m.
Madison, Alex Kimble, Old George, Donna Sykes and
Charlie Reach watched as Harley Weatherford
hurried in with a grocery bag in his arms. He
stopped there briefly to examine the group. He was
tall, extraordinarily thin with Raymond Burr circles
under deep set brown eyes and an undertaker's grey
skin.

"I apologize to you all then for my lateness," he
said formally. "However, one can never emphasize
enough the importance of breakfasting properly.

Some tea and a bit of seed cake should get us off to a jolly good start."

Minutes later Old George was grinning at the tidy wedges of cake on Harley's tray. "Didn't tell us we'd have a houseboy for this job, Madison."

"Joke if you must," Harley replied, pulling away the tray and offering it to the others. "I daresay you shall all be grateful to me later."

Madison smiled. "This is Harley, everyone. Harley meet Donna, George, Alex and Charlie."

Harley shook everyone's hand kindly, then turned back to Charlie. "You look *awfully* familiar, old boy. What is it exactly that you do for a living? In the real world, I mean."

Charlie Reach, Madison remembered, had retired or been dismissed from the field of Intelligence, no one was quite sure which. He always looked a bit grubby, wore small round spectacles, was at least a day behind on shaving, and Madison was convinced he had not cleaned behind his ears for quite some time. But she had seen Charlie put his bottle aside and sit for hours, sometimes days, studying a target, methodically recording every move, every idiosyncracy. She had watched him through a two-way mirror perform miracles in a bare interrogation room. Not by using force, of course. Charlie had once told her that sometimes force only served to bring out the rebelliousness in a person. Instead Charlie Reach, as a way of reeling his victim in, would become thoughtful and still. On more than one occasion Madison had seen these intervals go on for such an extended period of time that the person volunteered the information simply to break the tension.

Charlie smiled and answered Harley in his neat Scottish brogue between bites of cake. "I'm working on a piece of adventure fiction right now and just getting by, really."

Harley's eyebrows arched over his tea cup. "An adventure novelist, is it then?" he asked disapprovingly, for Harley Weatherford believed that such writers of fiction were lower in class only to street vendors and sidewalk painters.

"All right," Madison broke in. "I think we're ready, that is if I have your permission, Harley," she added dryly. "You've all been briefed. I don't have to remind you that you're expected to treat this with total secrecy. Donna will schedule our shifts, keep us organized and out of each other's way, and be our central contact. You'll turn in your reports to her at the end of your shifts. Together we'll try to zero in on our target. We have a list of possibles. We'll take them one at a time, watch their patterns, who they meet, who they talk to — "

"And generally invade their privacy," Old George broke in.

"That's about it," Madison laughed. "Now, Harley here will handle the listening devices, long range microphones, etcetera. George will take care of the photographs and video tape. Charlie and Alex will work on surveillance along with the rest of us." Madison walked to the fireplace, then turned to face the group. "The five of you have been selected because individually you're very good. But I beg you

35

all to remember that our success depends on our ability to function as a team. Rest up this afternoon. We start tonight."

Dan Wright took the escalator out of the Metro station towards the street, his hand around the small film canister in his pocket, his mind frantically reviewing the escape procedures all CIA case officers and operatives had rehearsed a thousand times ... Escape procedures they hoped they would never have to use.

The transfer on the train with Raven, Major Oleg Chenlovko's CIA code name, had been as smooth and professional as any Dan Wright had ever been involved in. So what had happened, he asked himself. *Why am I being followed?* Had they been watching the Major? Dan Wright himself? He had checked and double-checked to be sure he was not being tailed on the way to the subway station. He had been followed before but all Americans living in Moscow were routinely followed by the KGB, and on the days when he had been tailed he had merely given his contacts the wave-off signal by removing a glove or tying a shoe. But today he had detected no surveillance. At least not until it was too late ... Not until he had the evidence of his spying in his pocket.

He had to get to the street, had to get away from them and get rid of the film, rip it from its housing, expose it to daylight as he had been trained to do.

He turned casually, lighting a cigarette, and

glanced at the man in the coveralls and the old brown coat who was following him. The man had moved to within five meters. Dan Wright's heart began to race. He looked towards the street, fighting the urge to run up the slow moving escalator. Remain calm, he told himself. Chances are the KGB officer is on a simple surveillance detail and didn't even see the transfer on the train.

The escalator moved sluggishly from the bowels of the Metro station and at last the street came into view. Dan Wright crushed out his cigarette on the escalator steps and wrapped his hand around the film case in his pocket, popping off its lid in preparation.

Then he saw two men standing at the top of the steps looking at him, their hands in the pockets of their coats. He cocked his head just enough to get a glimpse of the man in the coveralls behind him, moving ever closer.

His heart thumping, he leapt over the railing and shoved his way down the jammed escalator, turning when he reached the bottom to see the men fighting their way through the subway station, pushing slow-moving Muscovites out of the way.

A train was coming to a screeching halt. He worked his way to the center of the crowd, and stood very still next to a tall man. He looked straight ahead, his collar pulled close to his face. He could hear voices behind him, hear the commuters grumbling at being jostled by his pursuers, hear the KGB officers yelling their way through the crowds.

The doors hissed open and he felt himself being propelled onto the train, being thrust and elbowed by the crowd. He saw four of them standing in the station as the train lurched forward, still searching for him, and for once Dan Wright was glad for the packed Metro stations of Moscow, glad for the dismal commuters, glad for their rude indifference.

Red-faced and out of breath, he found a place to stand near an emergency exit and rested his head against the fiberglass wall, closing his eyes, his hand still grasping the film container in his pocket.

Thirty seconds later he felt a brush at his sleeve and heard the voice beside him. There were two of them, one stubby and round, the other tall with a hollow Russian face.

"You are under arrest, Mr. Wright, for the crime of spying against the Soviet Union," the tall man said, grabbing his wrist while the stubby man reached into his pocket for the film.


At CIA headquarters, Mitchell Colby stared in frustration at the wire from the Moscow Embassy. TROUBLE ON THE RAVEN LINE, it read. RAVEN CONTROLLER MISSING.

"Damn it," Colby muttered, then looked at his Deputy Director of Intelligence who had delivered the message. "What about Raven? You think he's playing both sides?"

Fred Nolan shook his head. "No indication of that."

Colby leaned back in his chair and sighed. "Close the Raven line completely and notify everyone. We have to assume that anything we had left in Moscow that Dan Wright was privy to is blown"

"You think he'll talk?" Nolan asked.

"Everyone talks, Fred. You know that. He won't have a choice."

"What about Raven?" Nolan asked.

The Director took the message in his big hands and placed it carefully in his middle drawer. "Send him a warning. That's all we can do. He knew the risks."

His black shoes clapped against the cobbled streets, his chin down to the cold night air, his hands tucked into the pockets of his fur-lined coat. A paddle steamer drifted lazily over the frigid waters of Lake Lucerne as he stepped onto the covered Chapel Bridge and headed towards the rendezvous point.

Inside the old *Kapellbrucke*, amber lights brightened paintings of medieval saints and street scenes, and the occasional tourist stopped to examine Lucerne's primordial history. It was here that he first spied her, so beautiful and so deadly, gazing at one of the paintings.

He stepped alongside her and casually looked at the painting as he spoke. "She's in Geneva now with her group. It's only a matter of time before they close in."

The woman turned to him. "Poor darling, you look so tired," she said with the empathy he knew she did not possess, her low, slavic voice barely a whisper in the night. "Are you not convinced that she will follow the trail?"

He looked around to be sure no one was watching and pressed an envelope into her palm.

"She'll come. But she's very perceptive. If it's too easy she'll know something's wrong."

She smiled, stuffing the cash-filled envelope into her jacket. "I will look forward to the challenge."

"This is not a game, Natasha. One mistake and I'm blown."

Her eyes, flickering in the amber light, were as dark and cold as onyx. "My dear," she said, wrapping her hands around the back of his neck and tiptoeing to whisper in his ear as if they were lovers on that bridge, "if she does not do what is expected, she can be eliminated as easily as the fat clerk. A simple puncture in the substernal notch will silence your great spy."


They could have been any couple driving one of Geneva's better neighborhoods in their green Volvo, Charlie Reach at the wheel and Madison McGuire in the passenger's seat.

Charlie slowed the car. "Sixty meters, Madison, there's a blue Mercedes on the left. A new addition. A woman, five-foot-six approximately got out of the car three hours ago. Henderson met her on the walk. They embraced and kissed. Harley listened in from the van and said it was damn embarrassing once they got inside." He increased his speed. "Okay, thirty meters on the right sits Harley and Alex."

They passed the brown van with tinted windows that was their listening post. "How about the conversation?" Madison asked.

"Well there's been damn little conversation,"

Charlie answered with a wily smile. "The woman's name is Carla. Donna ran a check on her. We have her home address and her employer. She's been vacationing with her sister, and our Mr. Henderson has done without for three weeks. That's about it."

"Anything come up about Lyle Dresser?"

"He told his girlfriend Dresser was a nice guy. Seemed very shocked by the murder." Charlie turned onto the next block and glanced at Madison. "Honestly, Madison, I don't think Henderson's our man. We've been on him for days now and he hasn't had a hair out of place. Harley's even getting attached to him, I think, but you know how watchers get."

Madison nodded. She understood. She had been there herself. Surveillance teams had been known to get attached to their targets, begin to like or dislike them, identify with them in some way, lose their objectivity.

"Let's give it another day," she said. "Signal Harley the shift is over, would you, Charlie? You up for the night watch?"

Charlie nodded. "Spent most of the day in the hotel sleeping and watching movies. I'm rested. Need a ride back?"

"No. I think I'll walk a bit."

Charlie pulled over and Madison stepped out. "Madison," he said, leaning over in the seat. "We'll lock onto the right one. Just give us some time."

She walked through the freezing night air, making her way towards the pedestrian bridge, passing ancient stone houses and neat little gardens white with frost. She headed towards Old Town, admiring the Cathedral of St. Pierre with its great Gothic tower, marveling that any building could stand so strong and steady for nearly six hundred years; then she wondered vaguely who St. Pierre was. She passed a cafe and smelled coffee and cigarette smoke, then saw the bridge and the Jet d'Eau, Geneva's four-hundred-foot water jet, spewing and hissing like a great, huge snake, its spray illuminated by shafts of pink and blue from the spotlights.

Standing on the bridge, she looked down into the dark water, remembering the conversation she had had earlier with William Ryan. Dan Wright was missing in Moscow, he had told her, probably blown — another casualty.

She let herself remember Dan Wright, remember his big, friendly smile that told the world he loved it, that drew people to him like flowers to the light. She remembered his complete dedication to his work, to his family, to his friends, to his agents, to every task assigned him. She remembered the fun they had had training together as new recruits, remembered the operation they had run together years later.

Berlin at the height of the Cold War. There had been rumors among the Intelligence community that a high-ranking East German in the military had the heart of a capitalist. For their assignment, Dan Wright and Madison McGuire were Mr. and Mrs. Robert Eastlake. Dan Wright played the part of an American diplomat assigned to the consulate's political office, Madison his ever-faithful, ever-smiling diplomatic wife, engaging in small talk at dinners, watching the other wives in their low-cut gowns and their exposed cleavage, and reminding herself all the while to look at her husband with adoring eyes. And h e *was* shining, Madison remembered, charming them in his perfect German, telling bright jokes and occasionally glancing at Madison, holding his gaze on her just long enough, looking at her as if he had loved her all his life. He was spectacular, and Madison could not help but think that night that Dan Wright had missed his true calling of diplomat.

They had lived there for nearly four months. They entertained diplomats and military leaders, laughed and drank at diplomatic happy hours, and brunched with heads of State. They became friends, talking about their lives till then. Dan Wright liked to talk about his family. He loved his children and was still in love with his wife. He and Madison spent nights in the cipher rooms working the radios, sending out coded transmissions to their agents-in-place, and waiting impatiently for the big score. And when it came, when their job was over and they had turned an advisor to the East German military over to the West, their victory was bittersweet because they knew they might never work together again.

Since then, they had tried to keep in touch — a card here, a letter there — and only six months ago Madison had received a snapshot of Dan Wright's daughter at her high school graduation.

She sighed and pulled her coat closer around her neck. So many bridges till now, she thought as she leaned against the railing and watched the soft ripples in the water. So many cities, so many operations, so many friends lost.

Outside the safe house, the house the group had nicknamed Trace House, Madison leaned against the Volvo and lit a cigarette. The upstairs lights were off. Only a dim glow from behind the living room curtains gave any indication of the secret world within. If the upstairs lights were off, it meant Donna was not working in the computer room. But then what work was there to do at this point? Four days of watching Douglas Henderson from the embassy and not a scrap of worthwhile Intelligence. And before Henderson they had run checks on Lapp in Bern and Johnson in Zurich. Night Trace was moving at a crawl and the frustrations of the team were mounting. They had tried. God knows they had tried. Old George had installed his tiny lenses in everything from umbrellas to briefcases and photographed their surveillance subjects attending luncheons, meetings, going home and coming out again.

Charlie Reach watched and waited and watched and waited more, and once fell off the wagon in frustration over having no one to interrogate.

Donna spent hours at the computer, pulling up background files, checking travel schedules, credit card bills, bank accounts, searching in vain for the one selling secrets, in vain for the one buying.

And there was young Alex Kimble, female, black, dimples that lent a sort of natural happiness to her face, and inexperienced in the ways of the field. Madison had believed from the beginning that it would not be easy for Alex to join their team, to deal with the prejudices likely to exist. But Alex had carved out a spot for herself, taking to the streets with the patience and concentration of a professional, artfully shadowing the suspects, discreetly making inquiries after them. Alex had a way of making strangers comfortable with her questions, a natural ease when it came to striking up casual conversations. "My heart was going great guns," she confessed to Madison after her first time out, but she hadn't shown it.

And Madison did her best to help them all. She helped Harley devise ways to enter the homes and offices of CIA and embassy personnel with his clever devices. She worked in the makeshift darkroom at Trace House with Old George, talked Charlie down from his one drunk, joked with Donna and praised Alex. She shared with them their frustrations, their sense of failure, their sleepless nights. It was the money that had first lured them to Switzerland, she knew, but it was their own conscientiousness that kept them there, that had seen their moods swing from light to dark according to their hope for success. She had watched them blossom during operation Night Trace, watched them laugh and study and share stories and tradecraft, watched them adjust to each other's moods and learn to function as one cohesive unit, even with the startling differences between them. They wanted their victory and Madison wanted it for them almost as much as she wanted it for the Company.

She opened the front door quietly and heard

Donna Sykes' voice, the voice Donna used when she was weaving her tales and generally spreading Company folklore. Madison crept quietly down the entrance hall.

Alex, George, and Harley were gathered round her in front of the fireplace like adolescents around a campfire, excited and spooked all at once. Donna had them mesmerized, her face half-lit in the glow of burning logs, her voice so low and raspy she might have been talking about graveyards or men with hooks for hands.

But Donna Sykes was telling her own hair-raising stories, stories about the moles she had helped ferret out during her reign as head of Records, about tracing the steps of desperate women and men, about shadowy informants and double-crosses, all the while supplementing her own great memory for detail with her monumental imagination, which in Madison's opinion was part of her genius.

Madison leaned against the door frame, content to let Donna have her time center stage, watching as she teased them, strung them along, her voice rising and falling for effect.

"And then," Donna told the group, "she started the trek across Europe that's now legendary in the Agency, looking for the terrorist who set her up."

Madison smiled.

Harley Weatherford sat up in his chair, his brown eyes big with anticipation. "Go on then, Don," he pleaded. "What happened?"

Donna's intelligent little eyes gleamed in the firelight. She leaned forward and hissed, "Poison darts."

"Good evening," Madison said, stepping into the light.

Harley Weatherford leapt to his feet. "Dear God, woman. Scare the bloody hell out of us, will you. Give us some warning next time."

"Telling your stories again, are you, Don?" Madison asked. "Talking about anyone I know?"

"About you," Alex offered with her broad smile, watching carefully for Madison's reaction. It was not the first time Madison had been struck by the simple beauty of this young woman, not the first time she had felt that Alex's interest in her was beyond the merely professional. "Truth or fiction, Madison?"

"First lesson, Alex." Madison held up one finger. "Never believe anything that comes from anyone *ever* associated with the Company."

"And lesson two?" Alex persisted.

"Let's see." Madison thought seriously for a moment. "Oh, yes I have it." She smiled and reached for the open bottle of scotch on the table. "Never endure Donna's stories sober."

Old George laughed. "Well there you have it, grasshopper," he told Alex. "Your pearl of wisdom for the day."


In Buxton, North Carolina, Terry Woodall, unable to concentrate, pushed aside the paperwork she had brought home from her office.

She walked upstairs and paused at the study door, uncertain whether to go further. She had not been in this room uninvited since they had converted it from a spare bedroom to a sanctuary for her lover. It had been an unspoken agreement between them. Madison needed her solitude, needed this room as badly as she needed those furious morning runs, as badly as she needed to make love with Terry and then slip out of bed and creep into her study in the middle of the night where Terry would hear her pacing, hear her shuffling pages, hear her pen racing over the paper.

She had never seen anything written by Madison other than a card in the mail or a note on the kitchen counter. Madison never left papers around the house, barely left any evidence of herself at all. She wondered if Madison's writing was beautiful and tragic or clever and witty, wondered if it was a record of her work and her life till now, a life Madison rarely mentioned. She wondered if Madison burned it when she was done, or shredded it or stamped it Top Secret out of habit and locked it away somewhere. She remembered waking on so many mornings to find Madison standing over her, breakfast tray waiting, smiling, saying she had slept like a rock. She wondered how many trays Madison had carried in her life, to how many beds. For Madison was accommodating to a fault. Always willing to offer the reassuring words, the hug or the kiss. But never willing to tell you what was behind that smile.

There was so much locked inside her that at times Terry had wanted to grab her, demand, *Let me in*. But to expect secrets to come pouring out of someone who had spent a lifetime of training to keep them in was an exercise in futility. There was a part of Madison that would always be restricted even to Terry herself. It was a reality she was learning to live with.

She turned the doorknob, needing the comfort of seeing Madison's possessions in their home. The study was neat and organized the way Madison liked things. A battered copy of John LeCarre's *The Spy Who Came In From The Cold* lay on the desk. Terry picked it up and smiled at seeing the folded back pages marking the passages Madison either especially liked or had found something in common with. There was a framed picture of the mother who had died, her arm around the waist of Madison's father, the first spy in the family. A typewriter holding a clean sheet of paper, an ashtray that had been wiped clean, and on the desk pad a single handwritten note that read: Remember T's Christmas present.

Terry sat down in Madison's desk chair and ran her fingers over the note gently.

# — 4 —

In a shaky Krushchev-era apartment building, Misha Tikhomirov, twenty-four, slipped into his ill-fitting winter coat. His wife, Elena, had left hours ago carrying the two suitcases that held their personal belongings, headed for Tver, a village outside Moscow where she had cousins who would hide them. What would become of the others, Misha did not know. They had all planned for this, all worked out their escape routes long ago with no one knowing the other's plans.

The message had been delivered last evening

while Elena stood over a pot of boiling chicken that had cost her four hours in line at the Universam. It had been a good shopping trip. There was meat in the government grocery store, and candy, a rarity in Moscow, and Elena had bought the maximum allowed, one kilo. Misha was not home when the knock came and Elena did not want to answer, afraid it was the landlord coming to collect the nineteen rubles they owed for the month. But the caller was persistent, the knock quiet but steady and determined.

Elena did not recognize the face at the door, but the message was clear enough. "Misha must notify the black bird. It's time for us to go," the visitor whispered, then disappeared down the dirty hallway.

This was not a warning, Elena knew, not some vague suspicion that the network was being watched. This meant total collapse. It was the message they had all dreaded, the message that signified imminent danger.

Misha sighed and took a last look around the two-room apartment to be sure nothing was left behind that could lead the authorities to him and his wife or friends. They had gone through everything last night, destroying even their Democratic Party cards and snapshots of friends in an effort to leave no trace of their lives in Moscow or the disassembled network they had belonged to. They would never see those friends again, never see the other members of the underground network funded by the Americans. It was all part of the agreement. If ever the message came, they had agreed, they must never ever have any contact again.

He buttoned his coat and walked out the front entrance at ten a.m.

Ten-thirty a.m., opening time for Moscow bars. Major Oleg Chenlovko emerged from his apartment and walked towards his favorite bar, ready for his morning vodka, his pickled cucumbers and black bread.

The morning sun had melted the pavement snow and Chenlovko joined the Saturday crowds, opting to leave the official black Volga behind. He ambled through the slush, in no particular hurry, thinking about the Americans. He wondered how pleased they were after the last transfer, imagined them singing his praises in their high offices. Raven saved our man. Raven is our future in Moscow.

Oleg Chenlovko had no way of knowing that the intelligence had never made it out of the city, that his American controller had been arrested with a roll of unexposed film in his pocket and now sat in a KGB cell behind the Lubyanka.

"Welcome, Comrade Chenlovko," said the middle-aged man behind the bar. "Your table is empty. I'll bring your order right away."

Chenlovko strolled importantly to the booth and tossed his coat on the back of his seat. He did not notice the younger man slumping over his mug at the bar who had turned to watch as he walked past.

Chenlovko opened his copy of *Pravda* and went to the back page. It was a habit that came from living in Russia. The real news never made the front pages. He was half through his first vodka when he saw the young man approaching, obviously drunk, wanting money or trouble. Chenlovko would send him away without either, he decided.

"A beautiful morning, Comrade," the man slurred loudly. "A morning to love Mother Russia."

"Yes, yes." Chenlovko nodded and snapped the paper in front of his face. It was then that he heard the crash of the mug on the floor and looked down to see his boots splattered with beer.

The young man was retrieving a cloth from the bar hurriedly, apologizing. As he ran the cloth over the Major's boots he looked up and for the first time Chenlovko saw his eyes. They were crisp grey and clear. Not the eyes of a drunk.

"Anna says it's time for the Raven to fly," the younger man whispered. "Good luck, *dos vidanya.*"

Nine little words, words he had learned so long ago, words he hoped he would never hear. Over a puddle of beer on the floor of a filthy bar they had come like nine sharp blows to his stomach.


It was nearly three a.m. Madison had dozed off on the couch, Alex in the chair, George on the floor. Harley Weatherford returned from the kitchen and discovered Donna Sykes missing. He found her upstairs at the computer.

"You're supposed to get some rest before the trip tomorrow," she said, barely looking at him.

He made a grand sweeping gesture with one long arm and lowered himself to the floor. "To hell with the trip. Just another dead end, is what I say. One bloody suspect left on Madison's list and not a chance in hell he's our man."

Donna shook her head. "You're drunk."

"Really, Don," Harley continued. "Just think about it. This guy Richard Ward runs his agents from the best territory in Europe, and he's got a good cover running that little cleaning business. For a field man it's like falling into a tub of butter. I hardly think he'd let *that* go sour. Besides he's too low level. Probably couldn't get his hands on the kind of stuff that's getting out. And so what if we don't find the nasty bugger we're looking for anyway?" he asked bitterly. "It's not going to harelip the whole bloody world, is it then? Oh, I know Madison would say national security or save the bloody USA or something equally preposterous. But if one was realistic about it one could say that we're dealing with nothing more than a lot of spooks and generally shady characters here. Not exactly people to care about. How they all bore me."

Donna Sykes laughed. "Just what in the hell do you think *you* are, Harley? You and your creepy little electronic devices, listening in on bedroom conversations and morning visits to the bathroom."

Harley Weatherford sat up and for a moment an expression of real hurt crossed his drunken face. He fell back and announced haughtily, "Electronics is a very specialized field, you know. Above all that dark cloak and dagger. Now here I am in Switzerland with the lot of you because some stupid little clerk got an ice pick in the chest."

Donna Sykes leapt from her chair. "An ice pick,"

she repeated. "A goddammed spike. Why the hell didn't it register?"

The sheer magnitude of her discovery had set her on fire. Her eyes teared and her body tingled as if she were sniffing out a buried treasure. Her nimble little fingers moved with dexterity over the keyboard as she cross-referenced method files, foreign agent files, the files of Intelligence brokers. She smiled as she worked because she herself had written most of the files years ago. God, I'm good, she reflected self-indulgently, as the screen lit up and the printer began to whine.

Harley had summoned the rest of the group by now. Alex and George sat in kitchen chairs they had brought from downstairs. Harley, practically asleep on his feet, double-clutched a cup of tea. Madison smoked her brown cigarettes and hovered over Donna restlessly. Trace House had come alive again.

"There she is, Madison. That's our buyer. Vladov, Natasha Vladov. Five-foot-four, one hundred and five pounds, brown hair and eyes. Not bad, huh?" The group gathered round and studied the image on the screen. "She came on the scene just as I was leaving the Company," Donna resumed. "That's why it didn't come to me right away. Born in Czechoslovakia, trained mostly in Novgorod. She's a killer with no particular allegiance to any one country and apparently no political agenda of her own. She brokers information and kills for anyone who will pay her price." Donna turned to Madison. "She's been known to use a wide variety of semiautomatics, even dabbles in explosives. But she prefers manually utilized weapons. Spikes, knives, anything quiet for contract hits. It was the spike that made me remember. She's used it before."

"Dear *God*," Harley exclaimed, his face the color of ash. "That is the most disgusting thing I've ever heard."

Ignoring Harley, Madison gave Donna an appreciative pat and turned to the group. "We'll head for Lucerne in a few hours and start the surveillance on Richard Ward. If we can link him to Vladov, we'll know he's our leak."

"And if we can't?" Harley interjected.

"We'll have to start from the other end, let Vladov lead us to the mole."

"Now look here," Harley objected. "I didn't sign up to go against some bloody mad psychopath. You said this was a simple surveillance operation. I *heard* you say that."

"Shut up, Harley," Old George answered crossly.

Madison took Harley's arm and walked him to the door. "No point in getting everyone upset, is there, Harley? Now go get some rest. Things will seem much brighter after a few hours sleep."

She watched as the team filed out of the room. "Don," she said thoughtfully, "why do you think Langley's analysts didn't pick up on Natasha Vladov?"

"It's all a matter of asking the right questions," Donna Sykes replied proudly. "You can have all that information at your fingertips but if you don't know how to access it it's worthless. Besides, we've used her too, Madison. I remember the file. It was over my clearance level but I had my sources. They've probably buried her file so deep the analysts can't get to it."

Madison walked to the window. The street outside was covered with a fresh layer of snow. An old yellow lorry was limping up the incline, its engine sputtering, wheels spinning. Madison watched it absently for a few moments, then rested an affectionate hand on Donna's narrow shoulders. "Outstanding work tonight, Don, really."


The message had caught him badly off guard. His steps faltered when he rose to leave the bar and he felt the bartender's hand at his elbow, saw the bartender smiling, asking if he felt all right, if he had been ill. Half of Moscow was sick, Chenlovko heard him say through the panic that had clamped down around his temples and chest like an animal trap. He stepped onto the sidewalk and leaned against the building, closing his eyes for only seconds, just long enough to steady himself.

Think, think. What did it mean? The message was a Level One emergency, Chenlovko knew. The man had used Anna's name, the woman who had turned him so many years ago. It meant he could be blown already. No warning, no notice, no time for preparation. It was over, his life changed forever.

He pulled his collar up around his face and started up the street. There would not be much time now. They would send a few plainclothes security men to collect him quietly. No publicity. His records would be destroyed, his files deleted from the computer. No one would know Oleg Chenlovko had ever lived, ever betrayed his country. His neighbors would be given a story about his leaving so rapidly, a promotion, a transfer. Chenlovko knew how they worked. He was one of them.

He checked his pockets. Fifteen rubles. More than most in Moscow had saved, but not enough to save him now. He needed help. He tried to calm himself and remember the telephone number he had been given by his American controller, the number he was to use only in Level One emergencies.

He found a public telephone and waited impatiently in line. Lines, lines everywhere. Was there no place in Moscow without lines?

"Please," he told the heavy woman in front of him. "This is most urgent. I must go next."

But the woman merely folded her arms and rooted her fat little feet firmly into the pavement. Her stolid expression made it very clear that she intended to go nowhere. Russian obstinateness, he thought, reaching into his wallet and removing the blue Party card with the special insignia in the corner that identified him as a member of the KGB.

The booth was emptying now. Two teenagers came out wearing heavy beads around their necks and patched black market blue jeans. Chenlovko shifted his official glare onto the woman. "Move now or find yourself in the Lubyanka by nightfall." Fearfully, she stepped aside.

He dialed the number, heard a loud tone, then silence. "I am called Raven," he said quietly. "I'm in trouble. I need to talk to Oscar. I have to come in. Do you know who I am."

The American voice answered only, "Hold on."

The Major took a deep breath and looked outside. The woman was watching him, loathing him with

58

her eyes. I'm one of you, he wanted to tell her. Don't hate me. I was doing this for you.

And then the voice returned. "I'm sorry, you have no instructions."

The line went dead.

# — 5 —

This will do nicely, Madison decided, as she and
Alex Kimble surveyed the large A-frame that sat in
the hills overlooking Lucerne, surrounded by rented
villas filled with skiers and honeymooners and locals
who kept their blinds drawn.

Fred Nolan, Deputy Director of Intelligence, had
told Madison the house had been purchased some
years ago and was now used several times a year,
but not for any official purpose, even though its bills
were logged under safe house expenses. Madison had
not wanted to know when it was purchased or who

paid the upkeep, but Nolan volunteered the information, then became so defensive he might have been justifying its value to the finance department. Her sole interest in the house, she explained to him, was in how frequently it was used and to confirm that it had been used by many different people, for she wanted no problems with neighbors who might become suspicious at seeing new faces.

So now this gaudy government vacation spot, with its mirrored windows, marbled baths, wide screen televisions and bedrooms built on the sides so that it looked like a huge bird with its wings spread for gliding, had become the operational base for Madison and her group of specialists.

She pressed in the security code, watched the door lift, and drove the leased Mercedes into the garage.

"It could be worse," Alex said, smiling at Madison as they stepped into the house.

It *had* been worse, Madison reflected, especially in the early days. Those unforgiving nights in West Berlin, watching her freezing breath hang in the air like clouds of smoke while she waited to see if the agent she was running would make it through the checkpoints and across the bridge to freedom. Tiny flats in England where she had struck deals with members of the London underground and then listened as the disapproving landlord, who took her duties very seriously indeed, lectured her on the evils of associating with all forms of human debris. Long nights spent in automobiles on surveillance operations, tapping out tunes with a pencil against the dash to keep herself awake. So many different names on so many passports, so many names that her own name seemed strange at times. And not very long ago, that grimy hut in a Bekaa Valley terrorist camp.

"The others won't be here for a while," Madison said. "Pick a room, put your things up and we'll get started."

They started with the computer. Alex at the keyboard and Madison behind her. "Richard Ward is supposed to be in Zurich today," Alex reported, looking at the agent's schedule.

Alex felt the gentle brush at her shoulder as Madison pulled up a chair beside her, felt the distance narrow between them. She was always alert to Madison, aware of Madison's proximity to her in the room, Madison's strong, bony hands, Madison's scent. Madison leaned forward and in the light of the screen Alex saw her face in profile, saw the sharp jaw line, the straight nose, the shock of red hair against her forehead . . .

"Alex." Madison had said it twice before she heard. "Get the number at Ward's store. We'd better give a call and be sure he's gone."

"Right," Alex nodded.

They heard the rumble of an engine and Madison went to the window. Donna Sykes and Harley Weatherford had arrived in the brown van. "Well, there's two more of us. I'll open the garage and let them in. Make the phone call, will you, Alex?"

Harley got out carrying two magnetic signs which advertised a lock and key company. "Will this do, then?" he asked. "We've got three more sets inside, one for dry cleaning, one for laundry pick-up and one for plumbing."

Madison appraised the signs. "Very nice."

Donna Sykes, in jeans and a T-shirt, came around the van complaining, "What the hell do you need with three suitcases, Harley? You've been in the same sweater since I met you."

Harley grabbed his bags protectively. "I do not expect a woman of your stature to understand the need for personal items that make life bearable for someone like me. I've been forced into living like a vagabond with you people."

Donna tilted back her head and spat, "*Ha,*" which seemed to infuriate Harley and sent him stomping towards the door.

She gave Madison a bright smile. "Harley's been a little prick all day."

Madison frowned. "Yes, well don't be too hard on the old boy. He's really very good at what he does, you know. Just a touch eccentric at times, and perhaps a bit misunderstood."

Donna shook her head and blew out air like cigarette smoke. "Get real, Madison. He's a shit and you know it."


George parked the listening post, with its magnetic signs on the door advertising *Beltz Lock and Key Company,* across the street from Alpine Dry Cleaning. Madison and Harley sat in back facing a wall of communications equipment.

"Here she comes," George announced, when he saw Alex and Charlie pull up in front of the cleaners. "Thirty seconds she'll be in."

Madison and Harley put on the headphones in time to hear Alex talking to the woman at the counter. "I'd like these laundered. Starch in the collars. How soon could I have them?"

Madison dialed a number and within seconds they heard the beeps of Alex's paging system, and heard Alex tell the woman, "I swear, I can't slip away for a minute. Is there a private telephone I could use for a second?"

Madison and Harley exchanged smiles. "She's steady as a bloody rock," Harley said.

They heard Alex's footsteps down the short tiled hall, heard a door open and close, heard her whisper into the microphone pinned under her collar. "Okay, I'm in. It's not much of an office though. Kind of small and bleak."

"Just bug the bloody thing and get out," Harley shouted, even though Alex could not hear him.

"Damn. It's a standard single line phone," Alex reported. "It'll have to be modified to pick up conversation in the room. I'll have to bypass the hook switch. It'll take a couple of minutes."

George had his binoculars out and was watching the woman at the counter. "She just turned and looked towards the office. She's getting impatient."

"Radio Charlie to go in and keep her busy," Madison told Harley. Seconds later Charlie was stepping out of the Mercedes and heading inside the cleaners.

"Okay," Alex announced finally. "It's done. Think I'll check out his drawers while I'm here."

Beads of perspiration were forming around Harley's hairline. "No, you fool," he shouted to the wall. "Just get out of the blessed office."

"*Shit.*" It was Old George's voice, this time from the front of the van. "I think it's Rich Ward come home from his trip. Looks like the pictures of him. Coming down the walk, Madison, twenty meters behind the Mercedes."

Madison was out the side door of the van in an instant. She intercepted Richard Ward just outside the front door of the CIA-owned dry cleaners. "Could you tell me which road leads to Interlaken?" she asked him in German.

"Damn," Harley muttered. "Alex has gone quiet on me. What's happening, George?"

"Madison's got Ward away from the store. He's pointing like he's giving directions. Okay, here we go. Alex is coming out of the office."

When Harley heard Alex thank the woman for the use of the telephone, he took a deep breath and removed his headphones.

Alex Kimble passed Richard Ward and Madison McGuire on the street without even a glance in their direction.


The case against Richard Ward seemed to be building nicely. They had all managed to find reasons to hate the man. On a cobbled boat landing in Zurich they listened with a parabolic microphone while Ward explained to an unhappy informant that his fee had been reduced considerably. Langley had reason to suspect that his Intelligence was unreliable, Ward told him. But in trying to verify that information, the team found that the informant's fee had held steady at five hundred francs for quite some time. Richard Ward was pocketing two hundred and fifty francs for himself.

He padded his expenses by listing trips he never took. He sent in phony Intelligence that came from contacts he never made. He underpaid his agents and spent his money in bars where bartenders knew him by name. He talked too much and too loud. His sexual encounters were frequent and indiscriminate and he pursued them with amazing vigor. After a week of surveillance the team was near total exhaustion.

But it wasn't until the eighth day that Richard Ward gave the team something to hate him for besides his total incompetence.

Madison sat in the Square where Ward liked to eat lunch, her hair colored chestnut, her dark-rimmed glasses giving her a distinct scholarly look. She wore headphones and a small radio hooked to her belt while she read a book. Old George drove a taxi and parked outside the Square with Alex as his passenger. Charlie was stationed in the van across the street, Harley in the back.

Madison watched Richard Ward over her book as he started towards his favorite park bench. Then she heard Harley's excited voice coming through her headphones.

"Behind you, Madison, forty meters. A woman wearing jeans. Looks like pay dirt, old girl."

Madison adjusted herself casually on the bench. Natasha Vladov was on a collision course with Richard Ward. She spoke quietly into her microphone. "Start shooting now, George."

Harley's voice again. "Christ, Madison, look at her hand. She's going to give him the spike, isn't she?"

"I don't think so," Alex Kimble responded from the taxi. "Looks like a pass coming up to me."

Vladov glided towards Ward with the grace of a dancer, barely brushing against his sleeve. "You were right, Alex," Madison whispered. "I think we've found our mole. She put something in his left hand pocket. See what you can do to retrieve it, would you, Alex? Good work everyone."

Madison watched Natasha walk out of the park with the appreciation one professional gives another. Vladov never slowed, never looked back.


Moscow's wide, dim streets at dusk: part fable, part dream. A place to hide, to sink into the shadows. Unless you were one of the hunted. Chenlovko stumbled out of the telephone booth. No instructions, the American had said. *My God! They've cut me loose. They're afraid to come for me, afraid to help. But if I could get to them, maybe . . .*

He needed an automobile. The streets were too dangerous. He turned and headed towards his apartment, knowing his time was running short, but believing too that they would not come for him so early. No, they would come stealthily in the middle of night while there was no one awake to witness the arrest.

The black Volga was parked in front of his apartment building. He stepped in a doorway on the other side of the street and found his keys. The snow had started again. Big flakes coating windshields and concrete steps, piling up on the hoods of parked cars. And then he noticed it — the automobile halfway down the block, the snow melting on the hood as fast as it fell. The engine is warm, he thought. He watched for a moment, saw the windshield wipers make a single pass, glimpsed the two dark shadows in the front seat. His breathing nearly stopped and he flattened himself against the doorway.

An older man came into the entrance where he stood, a canvas grocery bag in his arms. He looked at Chenlovko strangely. *He sees my fear. He knows something is wrong. He'll call the militia.*

Chenlovko pulled out his Party card once again. "Move along, Comrade." Voice normal, official. "Surveillance operation."

The man did as he was told without question. The citizens of the Soviet Union were accustomed to being spied upon by their security police. The new leadership had promised the practice would soon stop. Chenlovko had his doubts.

He turned up his collar, affected a slight slump and stepped back into the street. His mind was racing. Where could he go? What would he do? No friends. Only political contacts or KGB. No lovers who could be trusted and his gun in his apartment. Gone forever.

He was passing the Arbat theater, looking at the young people in line for an American movie when he thought of the small apartment ten minutes by trolley from the Kiev Metro station. It had been so long ago, so many years. But it was possible that she still lived there. People in Moscow didn't move around once they'd found a decent place to live.

"I'm looking for Anna," he said to the thin blonde woman who answered the door. "Is she here?"

"Who are you?"

"Oleg. Tell her Oleg is here to see her."

She looked at him, appraised him cynically, then decided to close the door.

Oleg Chenlovko blocked the door with one strong arm, pushed his way inside and grabbed her shoulders. "I must see Anna."

Suddenly she sensed the fear in him, sensed it the way a dog might. Not as something to be touched or seen but carrying its own scent. And Oleg Chenlovko was surrounded by it.

"Anna is dead. She was my sister," she said, looking into his panicked brown eyes. "I am Ludmila Mikailovna."

"No. Oh, no," he muttered, finding the wall for support.

She closed the door and took his arm. "You are half frozen and in trouble, I see. I'll get some tea."

He followed her to the tiny kitchen and sat down. "When?" he asked.

"Four years ago. Why have you come only now?"

"I knew your sister many years ago ..."

"I know who you are," she broke in. "You have a son in Leningrad, Oleg. He lives with our mother. He is very handsome."

"A son. I ... I didn't know."

"Drink your tea. My husband will come home soon. You must go."

"Can you help me?" Chenlovko asked. "Please." Then he said, "A son ..."

"My sister loved you very much," Ludmila

69

Mikailovna told him, her frank blue eyes studying him sadly. "It was for your safety that she never contacted you, never told you about your son. The movement needed you more."

"A son."

"I have an automobile. Sometimes I forget and leave the keys. It's just outside. Now go, Oleg, and good luck."


Dan Wright woke to the rattling of keys at the cell door. It was a different cell, he realized, when the guard flipped on the light from outside. He could not remember being brought to this one, could not remember much about the last few days. There were the two men on the subway who had arrested him after Raven made the transfer. Then there was a dirty cell and two brutal KGB interrogators. Soon after, daylight had disappeared completely from his life, time was lost. He had been allowed to sleep here and there for minutes, or hours, he was never sure how long, between sessions. And then they had come for him again, sometimes waking him for dinner, and less than an hour later for breakfast. He knew their techniques — confuse and disorient, weaken the subject until his only reality became his interrogators. He had been trained to resist those techniques, to let his mind grip onto one constant thought and not let go of it for the sake of his own sanity.

But then the doctor had come, a small, impatient man with round eyes and bad teeth. It was the third day, he guessed, and no one, no one had been trained enough to resist the chemicals. After that his memories were fragmented, surreal.

He checked his arms. Six punctures. *Jesus, I've spilled my guts.*

He watched the guard enter with a food tray, heard the guard tell him it was time for breakfast, but his stomach was still full from dinner. *Bastards.*

# — 6 —

He wore jeans, a coat with fur around the collar and his shirt-tail was partially untucked in front. Madison thought she heard him mumbling or singing to himself, she was not certain which. He was fair-haired, tall and trim, the kind of person who looks fit naturally, and when his drunkenness caused him to stumble, he laughed aloud.

"Please don't make a fuss, Mr. Ward," Madison said quietly, when she intercepted him near his front walk. "Turn very slowly and walk towards the Volvo, please."

Richard Ward seemed to sober up slightly during the drive. Old George and Madison escorted him into the house and found the rest of the group waiting, Donna perched on a stool near the bar, Alex on the couch. Charlie was behind a desk they had moved into the living room, for Charlie had told them he did his best work from behind a desk. Harley greeted them at the door.

Ward immediately took Charlie for the leader, and confronted him at the desk. "What the hell is this?"

Charlie might not have heard. He simply withdrew a yellow pad from the center drawer and placed it on the desk.

"Sit down, please, Mr. Ward," he requested mildly, from behind his gold-rimmed spectacles. "The first thing we need to do is take care of a few minor details. Will your clerk be opening the store in the morning?"

But Richard Ward did not seem inclined to sit. "Who are you people?" he demanded.

"I'd like you to call your clerk, please," Charlie instructed. "Ask her to take care of the store and see to your dog. Tell her you've been called out of town on a family emergency. You see, you'll be spending some time here and we'd like to clear up any loose ends in your absence."

Harley delivered the telephone to the desk and handed the receiver to Richard Ward. "Number?" he asked.

Richard Ward looked around the room angrily.

"You really are outnumbered, you know," Harley said. "I should think you realize your options are few at this point. Number please?"

Ward snatched the receiver and recited the number. The group exchanged relieved glances. It was their signal that Ward would give in, that he had already accepted their authority over him.

With the call made, Charlie looked down at his paper and began in a voice so mild he might have been telling a bedtime story. "On Friday the twentieth you met with an agent, code name of Felix, I believe. You paid this agent two hundred and fifty Swiss francs and reported the payment as five hundred francs. Is this correct?"

"Jesus Christ," Ward mumbled, looking around once again at the group.

Charlie continued. "On the twenty-third you produced validated boarding passes that listed you as being on a flight from Zurich to Berlin, a flight you never took. How did you get those stamped passes?"

Richard Ward sank slowly into his seat. "You're a bunch of head hunters," he said, quietly. "Goddamned agency watch dogs. Okay, look, I've got a girl who works for the airline. And maybe I've pinched a few dollars in agent's fees here and there. Who hasn't? Right?" He smiled nervously.

Charlie did not budge, did not even look up before he asked, "What business did you have in Town Square on the twenty-fifth?"

"No business. I eat lunch there sometimes," Ward answered, defensively.

Charlie nodded and George delivered the photographs to the desk. "We're not quite sure what to make of these photographs, Mr. Ward. Would you explain?"

Ward lifted one photograph. "Explain what?

That's me in the Square with a sandwich. Listen, if I'm getting the axe let's just get it over with."

"Keep going," Charlie said, looking up from his paper.

Ward lifted another photograph and smiled. "Nice," he said, looking at the first frame that included Natasha Vladov. He lifted another and his jaw went slack. "Hey, wait a minute. What the hell is this? She's putting something in my pocket."

"When did you first make contact with Natasha Vladov, Mr. Ward?"

"I don't know any Vladov and I've never seen this woman until that day in the Square."

Alex produced the note that she had fished from Ward's pocket that same afternoon on a crowded street as easily as Natasha Vladov had put it there. It read simply: TWO HUNDRED THOUSAND TOMORROW.

Richard Ward denied any knowledge of the pass or any connection to Natasha Vladov, and Charlie Reach sat there behind the desk, sometimes staring at his writing pad, sometimes peering over his spectacles into Ward's hazel eyes, but always speaking in the same bored monotone and pausing after each answer to make a note no one else could see. He asked the same questions again and again. How long have you been working with Natasha Vladov, Mr. Ward? What information are you feeding her? And Ward's answer was always the same. He had come to the park to eat lunch. He had never before seen Natasha Vladov.

The logs in the fireplace had burned to ash. Morning was breaking. The light was rushing through the mirrored windows and brightening the A-frame, and still Charlie asked his questions and still Ward produced the same answers while the team watched tiredly. But Richard Ward seemed to be unraveling. His blond hair was drooping and falling in sweat-soaked strands onto his wide forehead. His eyes were bloodshot and he was pacing, snapping his answers irritably.

"Tell me about the two hundred thousand dollars American that went into your bank account on the twenty-sixth," Charlie said finally when he was sure Ward was suitably exhausted.

Ward laughed. "I haven't had two hundred thou in my account in my whole goddamned life."

"This is a statement of your account activity in the last thirty days," Charlie said, pushing the statement across the desk, playing his final card. "I think it's time you told us the truth."

Richard Ward sat down and looked at the statement. "My God," he muttered, barely above a whisper.

"What information did you deliver in order to receive the two hundred thousand, Mr. Ward. Names of agents-in-place? Operations?"

But Ward wasn't talking. He fell back in the chair and for the first time the seriousness of the situation seemed to hit him full force.

Charlie Reach let the silence go on for quite some time before he put his pad on the desk and leaned forward. "We have you, Mr. Ward. We have the evidence of your duplicity in these photographs, in your bank account and in your blundering, thieving tradecraft."

Ward was pale as porcelain. "Are you in charge

here?" he asked quietly. "I have to know who's in charge."

"You're hardly in a position to make demands," Charlie responded dryly.

Ward was out of his chair again, moving towards Charlie. George started to get up but Madison touched his arm to keep him from interfering.

Ward grabbed Charlie's coat sleeve. "I have to know who I'm dealing with. I may need protection."

"My name is McGuire, Mr. Ward, Madison McGuire," she said, emerging from the shadows and letting Ward get his first good look at her in the light. "I take it you've decided to talk."

"I remember your face," Richard Ward said. "The street outside Alpine cleaners."

"Why is it you think you need protection?" Madison persisted.

"You're looking for a mole, aren't you?" he asked. "Well, I'm here because your mole is setting me up. He thinks I can blow him."

Charlie moved and let Madison have his place behind the desk.

Ludmila Mikhailovna's husband returned home, saw the automobile missing and worked himself into a rage by the time he entered the apartment because his wife would not be there to prepare his supper. His anger only increased when he pushed open the apartment door and saw his wife in the kitchen.

"Where is the car? Have you forgotten the keys again? Has it been stolen?"

"But I am sure I brought them inside this time," she answered meekly.

He said nothing, simply moved to the telephone and dialed the police to report the stolen Zhiguli. When he had finished, he turned to his wife. She knew what was coming next. He beat her often.

Oleg Chenlovko parked the yellow Zhiguli on a side street near October Square and fished in his pockets for the two kopecks needed for a telephone call. He dialed and said only, "This is Raven again. I'm coming in. I have no other way out. You must help me."

He replaced the receiver and turned in time to see the traffic police cruising by slowly. Quickly, he lifted the receiver and watched them while he pretended to be talking. The auto directorate vehicle stopped, one man stepped out and recorded the car number, then returned to the vehicle. Inside, Chenlovko could see the driver speaking into his radio. He knew it would be only minutes before more police arrived. He stepped away from the telephone calmly, turned up the collar of his coat and quickly sank into the cold shadows of a Moscow night.

Inside the American Embassy, Scott Larimer, Dan Wright's CIA replacement, rushed out of the political office. "Wire Langley. Rush, code red," he ordered breathlessly once he had reached the cipher room.

"Sorry, Mr. Larimer," the code clerk answered. "We're jammed. Nothing coming in or out. The Russians must have set up a transmitter somewhere in the area. Best I can tell they've pointed about a hundred thousand watts of scrambled junk at us. Can't even get a local television station."

"Jesus," Larimer muttered. "Can they intercept too?"

"Local calls maybe. That's all."

Scott Larimer sighed and lowered himself hopelessly into a chair. "Raven called back on the Moscow line, says he's coming in. They must have guessed he'd call, and if they've got Dan Wright they know who Raven is by now. *Shit.* They'll be waiting for him and there's not a damn thing I can do."


"Do go on, Mr. Ward," Madison instructed, turning to a fresh sheet of paper and picking up Charlie's pen.

"Seven weeks ago I was in Geneva to watch a delegation of Soviets who had come over for a convention," Richard Ward began, and Madison wondered if he had rehearsed those words. "American, German and Soviet scientists, all there to share some technological breakthrough. No big deal, I thought, just routine surveillance. Then I heard that Sergi Alexandrovich Novgorok was one of them. Novgorok was one of the scientists they'd put in the slammer for a while, one of the peace crowd. He's been quiet ever since. But I figured a guy like that doesn't just suddenly change his politics. I knew it wouldn't be easy to get to him with all the KGB they send with these guys, but I figured I could really score if I did. But Novgorok wasn't like the others. They all went out to this trip joint every night, the Ba-Ta-Clan. But Sergi just went to his meetings, took a couple of walks a day and stayed in his room with the baby-sitter next door. So I hired a prostitute to make some noise in the hallway, get the baby-sitter out there and come on to him. Well, the guy went for it and I headed for Sergi's room.

"I lied about my name. But everything else I told him was the truth. I said I was CIA and I could probably set up an escape providing he was willing to work with us." Ward paused and smiled, and his greedy hazel eyes came to life again. "You should have seen this guy. He didn't believe me, thought I was KGB setting him up. But the more I talked about America the more he came around and pretty soon he was holding onto my hand like I was the fucking Savior and I was thinking how lucky I was to hit him when he was ripe. He was just busting to talk — "

"How did you get into Novgorok's room?" Madison interrupted.

"I picked the lock. How would you get in?"

"Do go on."

Ward rubbed his hands together nervously. "Okay, we're in the room. I can hear the thug next door huffing and puffing for all he's worth and I know he's not gonna last long, so I tell Sergi about a letter drop I use sometimes. I tell him if he can give us a taste of the stuff he could give the West, it might help guarantee him a nice, big house in Montana."

"Where is this drop site?" Madison asked without emotion.

"The Rue du Rhone where Sergi liked to take his walks and look in the shop windows. A little newsstand."

"And when you spoke with Novgorok what language did you use?"

Ward laughed. "English mostly. My Russian's shaky. I think that actually helped me. A member of the KGB couldn't speak Russian that bad. So anyway, the next day I hang back while he takes his walk with his baby-sitter in tow. I see him stop at the newsstand and pick up a magazine, check it out and put it in the back of the stack. Then he buys a newspaper and moves on like he's been making drops all his life."

Ward was talking so fast that his lips were whitening and sticking to his teeth. Madison asked Old George for a glass of water and watched Ward as he drank.

"I wasn't prepared for what he left at the drop," he continued. "Two pages front and back on hotel stationary. *Beau Riuage*, it said on the top in gold letters. Novgorok said the Soviets have a deep penetration agent in the CIA they've been priming for like fifteen or twenty years. The mole's working name is Bradford and he's run by a Soviet agent in D.C. whose cover is Commercial Attache."

Madison folded her arms across her chest. "Mr. Ward, how do you explain a scientist having access to this kind of Intelligence?"

Ward colored slightly and raised his voice. "His brother-in-law is a code clerk in one of the Moscow code rooms. This guy told Sergi that Bradford sends over so much stuff it takes two clerks fifteen hours a week just to decode it."

Madison glanced over Ward's shoulder at Donna — a silent order to pay close attention. "Did Sergi write his brother-in-law's name in the letter?"

"Vitrolkov, Pyotr, I think," Ward answered.

Seeing Donna's nod, Madison made a note. "And did his letter also give you the name of the Commercial Attache?"

"His name is Krasavchenko, Dmitri Krasavchenko." He began spelling the last name. "K-r-a-s — "

She glanced at Donna who was again nodding her silver head enthusiastically. Madison's green eyes moved back to Ward and swept over his face deliberately. "You remember this letter very well."

Charlie smiled and elbowed George approvingly, as if he had taught Madison everything she knew.

Ward was up and pacing again. "You're goddamned right I remember it. I spent the whole fucking night coding it letter for letter, word for word to send to Langley. You don't forget a thing like that. Novgorok was the biggest fish I ever caught. I mean I contacted a Russian scientist on a hunch and reeled the bastard in. It was unbelievable."

"You drink quite a lot, don't you, Mr. Ward?" Madison asked coolly.

He shrugged. "I don't know. I guess so. What's that supposed to mean?"

Madison did not answer. Instead she consulted her notes and began, "At any point, did it occur to you that the recruitment of Sergi Alexandrovich Novgorok was a bit simple?"

Ward sat back down and looked at her seriously. He spoke without defensiveness, understanding the legitimacy of her question. "Oh yeah, I thought about it, worried about it being a trap, Novgorok being a misinformation plant. But then I just kept seeing his eyes and the way they looked at me that night. The only light was coming from the street and I couldn't see them until he sat up. They were green." He pointed at her. "Not your green, more brown, and kind of dull at first. Then he started to believe me and they got reckless and excited like he'd found Jesus or something. I'll never forget those eyes." He turned to the group. "You know what it's like," he said with the desperateness of a man who needed to be believed. He swung back to Madison. "You've brought them over before, haven't you?"

Madison was silent for nearly a minute, and just briefly Alex thought that perhaps Ward's question had shaken loose something from the past and brought it to the forefront of Madison's memory, for Madison's eyes seemed to be fixed on some point beyond that room. Alex looked at the others. Harley stared at his feet. George folded his arms over his chest and sank down into the couch. Charlie rambled into the kitchen. Donna closed her eyes. And suddenly Alex Kimble felt very much like an outsider in this secret society, knowing that the shared experiences of the group had linked them somehow, had provided them with a kinship, a silent rapport that came only with years of experience.

"You said you coded a copy of the letter," Madison said at last. "What code did you use and how was it posted?"

"I used a code pad I'd been issued a few weeks

back. I marked it: *decipher urgent — waiting response.* Then I waited for eight and a half hours on pins and needles at the Geneva station. When the response came it said: *abort — source unreliable.*"

"I see. And when you cabled Langley did you tell them everything you've just told me?"

"You better believe it," Ward answered, shaking his tired head in frustration. "Everything. How I met Novgorok, how he wanted to come over, and I still got an abort."

"And did you abort?" Madison asked quietly.

"Reluctantly, yeah. But I don't believe Novgorok was unreliable just like I don't believe he had a heart attack like the papers said the next day." Madison looked up from her notes. "That's right," Ward nodded. "He's dead."

Richard Ward must have felt the tension in the room at that moment. For three full minutes there were only the sounds of waiting — Charlie's soft-soled footsteps coming from the kitchen, the rustling of the sofa cushions when Alex sat forward, the wheel striking the flint of Harley's cigarette lighter.

"Where is the original letter Novgorok gave you?" Madison asked, so still she might have been listening for some distant voice. Every set of eyes was locked on Richard Ward.

"I was afraid to carry it around so I had it put in the hotel safe," he answered. "By the time I got back to the hotel the clerk was gone. The manager told me there'd never been a manila envelope in the safe. I raised hell but it didn't do any good."

Madison put her pen down and lit a cigarette.

"You say this happened seven weeks ago. Why didn't you go to the Geneva station chief with your story?"

"He would have sent me to Langley, right? And considering what happened to Sergi, I figured I'd be a hell of a lot better off keeping my mouth shut."

Madison stood up. "Get some rest, Mr. Ward. We'll start over in a few hours."

# — 7 —

Mitchell Colby returned to work. He had been home for a day. It was a winter cold, he insisted, that made him feel so tired. He entered the building and went directly to the third floor situation room where he found Warren Moss, Fred Nolan and William Ryan standing in front of the walls of communications equipment, watching an image form on the big screen: the still photography of Natasha Vladov and Richard Ward taken by Old George in the Lucerne Square.

Fred Nolan smiled and turned to Director Colby.

His clothes were wrinkled, had obviously been slept in. "I have to admit, Madison and her group are doing some fine work."

"Welcome back, Mr. Colby," Warren Moss said. "Feeling better?"

But Mitchell Colby was in no mood for friendly chat. He walked to the coffee pot, removed the stained pot and filled his mug. "Who is it?" he asked, cocking his head towards the screen.

"Richard Ward," William Ryan answered, refilling his own mug. "From the Geneva network. The woman is Natasha Vladov, a former Czech agent. An independent now."

"Have they questioned Ward?" the Director asked, moving to the screen and studying the faces.

"They're in the middle of it," Warren Moss answered and then did his best British accent. "Madison says the man is utterly wretched with absolutely no redeeming qualities whatsoever."

Colby chuckled. "Half of our operatives have no redeeming qualities. Have they arranged a cover story for Ward's disappearance?"

Fred Nolan nodded. "We're calling it a family emergency. We've arranged it with the hospital where Ward's mother lives. It's on their records now. Shouldn't send out any alarms. Hopefully we can use Ward later."

Colby sat down and thought about that. "Running doubles is a tricky business. Hard on everyone, especially the agent. I wouldn't want to be in that rascal's shoes. I want the three of you dealing with Night Trace directly."

"Right," said Ryan. "We've arranged a computer link. They can access most everything they need from Geneva. Top priority, no tracers. We're skipping the cipher rooms and any communication from Madison goes straight to me or Fred or Warren. We've got a couple more analysts looking over what comes in, but it's all been laundered. They don't know what operation they're dealing with."

"Good," Colby answered, suppressing the persistent cough that had been nagging him for some time, and wrapping his freckled hands around his coffee mug for warmth. "This one's got to be kept quiet."

Madison McGuire gathered her group of specialists together in the den of the Lucerne house. Harley, superior in attitude, but a genius when it came to electronics. Old George, easy going and just happy for the work. Alex, young and bright and eager to succeed. Charlie, a bit muddled but lovable nonetheless. And Donna Sykes, the little actor, always hoping for a dramatic ending.

"I want to thank you all for the wonderful work you've done," Madison told them, and then added with a smile, "Bringing you together like this has been an experience I won't soon forget. Donna, I need you and Charlie to stay on a while. The rest of you are free to go. Use your Swiss escapes, please, and thank you again."

"What will you do now?" Harley asked. "About Richard Ward, I mean?"

"I'm not sure," Madison answered quietly.

Old George rose from the couch. "I say we string the rascal up."

Madison nodded. "I'll keep that in mind."

Harley passed by and kissed Madison's cheek. "I'm on the next plane out of here. Do take care of yourself." He looked to the others. "Hope you get that piece of fiction finished up soon, Charlie, old boy. Wouldn't mind reading over it. I'm in the London registry, by the way. If any of you are ever in the neighborhood. Goodbye then, and good luck."

Alex Kimble rose slowly and only after the others had gone off to pack. Madison touched her arm softly as she passed. "I need you back at Langley, Alex. I don't know where this thing is going. I may need a friend on the inside."

"I understand," Alex answered, smoothing the oversized sweater she wore, avoiding Madison's eyes. "It's just that I really like it out here, Madison. I *like* the field. I like working with you. I like being part of the team."

"We're not done yet. This operation is far from over."

Alex nodded and made her way out. "By the way," Madison said without looking up. "You were everything I knew you'd be, Alex. Good work."


An hour after they all shook hands and said their final goodbyes, there was a quiet tap at Madison's door. Charlie and Donna came in to find her sitting in the center of a bed strewn with photographs. "Leave the door open, please, in case Mr. Ward wakes up," she said, distractedly. "Wouldn't want him slipping out on us."

She went back to one particular photograph and

studied it closely. Natasha Vladov in the Square at the second the pass was made, frozen in mid-flight, one small foot leaning towards the toes, the other already into the next step. Blue jeans and a leather coat nipped at the waist. One gloved hand at her side, shoulders straight. One hand partially blocked by the fabric of Richard Ward's coat, eyes steady, looking somewhere ahead.

And there was Richard Ward, his sandwich bag in his hand, head tilted slightly forward, a half smile with no teeth visible, eyes on Vladov.

"Look at this," she said, motioning for Charlie and Donna. "Look at Ward's face. He's looking directly at Natasha, about to nod and smile maybe, or flirt a bit like you might with a stranger on the street. By the look of him I think there's a chance he didn't know she was putting the note in his pocket."

"Oh, good *Lord*, Madison," Charlie grumbled. "You don't actually *believe* his story. I mean look at what we have here. An absolutely deplorable man, a man all of us would like to see hanged, I'm sure." He held up his thick fingers and counted off his case against Ward. "One he's a liar, two he's lazy, three he's completely incompetent, and four he steals from his own agents. And we have all seen the evidence, after all. A hand off, a note found in his pocket, a bank deposit. Yes, I'd say it's a very neat little package against Mr. Ward."

"I'm not sure what to believe," Madison remarked quietly, walking to the window. Terry would have told her to follow her gut feelings, she thought, but then that was just like Terry, who pretended to be cynical while she wore her heart on her sleeve. Was it a gut feeling, that mysterious thing called instinct, that was telling her to use caution now? Or was it habit? After all, she had spent half her life looking for conspiracies, even when they didn't exist.

The sun was setting. She watched the people on the street outside, a young woman putting a package in the boot of her car, a man walking a speckled mongrel, a grey van parked near the curb. Had the van been there last night? *I'm seeing spooks in the shadows.*

"I'll get started right away checking out his facts," said Donna with sincere pleasure at the prospect of getting back to her burrowing. "The locations should be easy to verify — the hotel, the newsstand, the nightclub. He got Krasavchenko's name right. I remember when he came to Washington as Commercial Attache ... Wonder if they've kept his file current. Langley never did seem to worry about him much. I need to get a look at it."

"No," Madison snapped. "No checks on Krasavchenko. I don't want Langley to know what Ward's told us just yet. And, Charlie, no matter how utterly worthless he may be, we owe it to him to investigate every avenue fully."

Charlie shrugged. "We could put him on the box, you know. I've given a polygraph or two in my day."

Madison thought about that. "Yes, but it can be beat. I've done it myself. It's not difficult."

He smiled. "That was you, this is Rich Ward. The man has no control. You saw him last night. He was absolutely hyper at some points. Maybe he could beat it once, but if I tested him say two, three times, he wouldn't be able to maintain. He'd slip."

Madison nodded. "I'll ask for a machine."

The streets had emptied, the temperature and wind chills sending even the hardiest of Muscovites into their warm flats. Chenlovko knew time was short. They would find him or the wind would freeze him. But like a frightened animal, instinct was the overpowering force that drove him now, that kept him moving even as the cold cut through his boots and the snow froze on his eyelashes.

A taxi crawled through the snow down Gorky Street, Moscow's main thoroughfare, and Chenlovko stopped it only by running after it until he reached the driver's door and jerked it open.

The pudgy, bearded driver shouted angrily, "My shift is over. Go away, damn you. Close the door."

"Ten rubles," Chenlovko promised. "Ten rubles for a fifteen minute drive."

"Get in and show me the money."

Chenlovko climbed into the broken-down taxi and retrieved the money from his pocket. The driver nodded. "Where to?"

"The American Embassy," he answered solemnly, and turned to the window, silently saying his goodbyes to the Socialist winter, to the Moscow that had been home, school and refuge for him, to the Russia he had hated — and the Russia he had loved, even while he was betraying it.

His hopes rose when the taxi rounded the corner and he saw the embassy gates standing open like an invitation to freedom. And as they moved closer, the warm yellow lights from the embassy's ground floor caused his faith to soar, leaving the terror and isolation of the day behind him.

And then the blinding spotlights from two field trucks struck the taxi like a lightning bolt, and he heard the cracks of a hundred rifles shoved into their firing positions.

The driver looked at his passenger helplessly, teeth gaping through his dark beard, and Chenlovko had only enough time to murmur one last confession. "I did it for Russia," he said, swinging open his door.

Oleg Chenlovko had put one boot to the frozen ground when the line of militiamen opened fire.


"Your name is Richard Clark Ward." Charlie much preferred statements, and all their implications, to questions during a polygraph.

"Yes," Richard Ward answered, adjusting himself in the seat. "My father loved Clark Gable."

"You must be still, Mr. Ward," Charlie said in the same monotone. "You were born on October seventeen, nineteen forty-five."

"Yes."

"You were born November second, nineteen forty-five."

"No."

"You are now acting as a double agent."

Ward sighed. "No. I'm not a double. I told you that."

Charlie looked at the machine and then at Ward. "Just yes or no, please. You attended college at Colorado State University."

"Yes."

"You have been selling classified information."

"No."

"You know Sergi Alexandrovich Novgorok."

"Yes," Ward answered.

"Novgorok is your Soviet controller."

"No."

"You first met Novgorok seven weeks ago in Geneva."

"Yes."

"You know Natasha Vladov."

"*No.*" Ward seemed to be losing patience.

"You've been working with Vladov, haven't you, Mr. Ward. Yes or no?"

"No, goddammit. I don't know the bitch."


It was seven-thirty p.m. when Charlie finished with Richard Ward, when he had asked him every question ten times, then asked ten more for good measure until Ward's eyes began to glaze and Charlie felt like a hostage taker.

When Madison opened the door to let Charlie in the workroom, his face held the expression of a movie-goer after an especially disappointing feature. He plodded his way over the thick carpet to a corner chair, shoulders slumped, head down, his eyes pink-rimmed with tiredness. He paused, and for a moment Madison thought he was going to speak, but all that came out was a sort of slurred mumble. He sat down and cleaned his glasses with the tail of his shirt.

"Let's have it, Charlie," Donna urged. "Give us the news."

Charlie sat his thick spectacles on the bridge of his nose. "He's a liar, no doubt about that. Funny thing is he lies about the insignificant things. Like speaking Russian. The bugger's fluent." He shook his puzzled head. "One wouldn't think he'd lie about the little things at this point. I mean we've already established he's a scoundrel, haven't we?"

"The big things, Charlie. What about the big things?" Madison asked impatiently.

Charlie looked a bit sad. "If you mean is he spying for the Soviet Union, he is not. In fact he's doing damn little of it for anyone, and that includes the USA I might add. Nor has he ever known Natasha Vladov during his entire miserable little existence. And the story he told us did indeed come from the Russian scientist."

Madison and Donna looked at each other. "Where is he now?" Madison asked.

"Smoking, thinking, gazing out the damn door like a man on death row. He's frightened, Madison. He thinks Bradford is going to have him killed."

She was moving before Charlie had finished. *The van on the street, the grey van. My God, it's Bradford's people.*

She could see Ward as she reached the end of the hallway. He was exactly as Charlie had said, standing there in the doorway, staring, the glow of his cigarette streaking his face orange as he inhaled.

"Get out of the doorway," Madison yelled, running towards him.

It happened in an instant. Automatic weapons

erupted from outside. The mirrored windows exploded, bullets ripped into the walls, pictures blew apart, the chandelier crashed to the floor, a low painful shriek rang out from behind Madison, and she jerked around in time to see Charlie thrown backwards, his shirt splitting, a mass of dark red covering his chest.

"Ward," she yelled, crawling along the floor, trying to protect herself from the flying glass and the constant barrage of bullets, her 9mm in her hand.

"I'm here," he shouted from behind the couch. "Oh, shit, I've been hit."

Madison heard sirens in the distance. The automatic weapons stopped suddenly. *Now*, she told herself, and with a swiftness born of pure instinct, she raced through the open door and fired as Bradford's people were running to the van. She caught one of them in the back of the leg. His weapon flew from his hand but he kept moving. The other one, a woman, was already in the driver's seat. Madison had seen the long hair flying behind her as she ran, recognized the willowy figure, the fluid movements. Natasha Vladov. The passenger door flew open, the wounded sniper climbed in and the van raced away. Madison picked up the abandoned weapon, a Mac-10, and ran back to the house.

Richard Ward was lying on the floor, his hand covering his shoulder, blood trickling through his fingers. Madison pulled his hand aside and looked at the injury.

"It's not severe. Get to the van" she ordered hurriedly.

Richard Ward moaned. "It hurts."

"Move, Mr. Ward. *Now*. Or I'll kill you myself." She was up and running before he could speak again, yelling for Donna, the 9mm pistol in one hand, the Mac-10 in the other.

She burst into the workroom and Donna's small head popped up from behind the desk, her blue eyes wide and scared. "I heard shots." Her voice trembled.

"We've got to get out now," Madison told her, and turned to the computer. "We can't leave anything behind for the police to link with Langley. How do we clear the memory on this thing?"

"Reformat the main drive, erase some batch files. It'll take a few minutes. Jesus God, Madison, what's happening?"

But there was no time for explanations. "Jerk the connections and step back," Madison ordered, and when Donna was finished she opened up the Mac-10 and reduced the equipment to rubble.

Donna stood motionless, staring blankly at the shattered remains of her research.

"Hurry, Don. Come on."

They ran through the living room. But Donna stopped cold when she saw Charlie's mangled body on the living room floor. In a split second Madison had propelled her through the door.

The sirens were closer now, blaring up the street. Donna jumped into the passenger's seat. Richard Ward, clutching his shoulder, sat pale and silent in the back. "You're just going to leave Charlie — in there like that?" Donna stammered.

Madison crashed the van through the garage door and hit the street, tires screeching. "Charlie's gone,

Don." She jerked the wheel and spun around a curve, passing a line of police cars. "There's nothing we can do now."

Madison felt Donna's eyes on her. "We never really knew him, did we?" Donna said quietly. "I mean what kind of man he was apart from his work, if he had sisters or brothers, if he'd ever been in love."

Madison glanced at her. "I never asked, Don. You can't get too close. You just can't."

"Jesus, Madison, just listen to yourself. What kind of world do you live in?"

"It looks different from behind Company walls, doesn't it?" Madison was angry and she wasn't sure why. "It's so much cleaner when you're looking through a glass cubicle, so nice and sterile. We're the flesh and blood, Don, me and Charlie and all the others. We're the numbers you looked at everyday on your computer screen. Welcome to the *real* world."

The fog was gathering in thick pockets, drifting through the streets like ghosts, illuminated by the yellow light of the train station. Ward sat with his head back, eyes closed. Madison and Donna had been quiet for some time, both suddenly aware of the unbridgeable gap between the strategists who worked on the inside and the ones who actually practiced the craft on the outside.

Madison pulled to the curb. "We'll have to leave the van here, I'm afraid. Bradford's people will be looking for us as soon as they find out Ward's still alive." She looked in the rearview mirror. "Still with us, Mr. Ward?"

"Yeah. The bleeding's stopped."

"There's a coat back there. Wrap it around your

shoulders and wait in the station with Donna while I find a call box. You should be strong enough to walk a bit."

"I can manage," Ward replied, and then, "Madison, I really appreciate everything you're trying to do for me."

Madison spun around. "None of this is for you, Mr. Ward."

He was born in Dublin, and a decade later his father was killed in the War of Independence that won back the counties of southern Ireland from British control. When he was sixteen he was experimenting with improvised explosives and selling them to the underground. At twenty-six he was an active member of the Irish Republican Army, working for the reunification of southern Ireland and fighting to end British rule in six counties of Northern Ireland. At thirty his wife left him and when he was thirty-nine a car bomb made by his own hand killed a moderate spokesman for Ulster in the parking lot of the House of Commons. Max Rudger walked away from the IRA then, permanently disillusioned. After years of fighting and killing he had seen the organization's agenda growing, becoming more radical, more violent, moving further away from the initial goal of freedom for Ireland.

He was forty when he was first approached by a member of the Central Intelligence Agency, an agent named Madison McGuire.

Max and Madison had worked a dozen or more

operations together since then, from Ireland to Beirut, and he loved her as much as he had ever loved anyone in his life.

Now, at age fifty-five, Max Rudger sat quietly in front of the fire, his new wife's feet in his lap, rubbing them gently with his big hands, making small circles with his thumb on the tender spots. Helen had nurse's feet, he thought, hard and wide and very often tired. He sat peacefully with Helen in the light of the fire, and when the telephone rang and he stood to answer, he nicked his shin on the table and swore aloud.

His wife heard him speak softly into the phone. Soon he came to her. "It's Madi, darlin'. There's been some trouble. I'll have to go for her."

Helen knew he would always go for Madison, knew the bond between them was beyond her understanding. She got up from the couch and took his hand. "I'll put some coffee on."


Two hours later Madison McGuire and Donna Sykes were sitting in Max Rudger's kitchen on the outskirts of Zurich, a plate of cheese and salami sandwiches in front of them, Madison sipping coffee, Donna nursing a glass of Max's whiskey.

The farmhouse had not changed much since Max's second marriage. It was a bit neater perhaps, but Max, a bachelor of nearly twenty-five years, had learned how to keep things tidy long ago. There were a few new additions — cut flowers in a vase on the kitchen table, and the old red and white checkered curtains had been replaced by blue ones printed with a barnyard scene.

Helen came out of the spare room. She was blonde, blue-eyed like her husband, a good fifteen years younger, with a round china doll face.

"He'll be fine. The bullet just creased the shoulder," she said with the hint of a German accent, walking to Max and wrapping her arms around him from behind while he sat next to Donna Sykes at the kitchen table. He squeezed her hand softly, with the familiarity of a lover.

Madison couldn't help but smile at the sight of them. "I really am sorry about barging in this way," she said.

"Don't be listenin' to her, darlin'. She's always bargin' in," Max objected, giving Madison a wink. "What can I do for you, love?"

"We need passports," Donna piped in. It was the first time she had spoken since leaving Lucerne.

Max twisted up the corners of his mustache with his thumb and forefinger while he thought it over. "Oh, I can get the paperwork. I'm just wonderin' how in blazes the three of you got left with no papers, no vehicle, and one of you with a bleedin' bullet hole."

"It's a long story, Max," Madison answered. "I'll tell you everything tomorrow, but tonight we're exhausted. Can you put us in the bunkhouse?"


He answered the telephone nervously. His secretary had said the call was from a doctor named

101

Vernon. It was the prearranged code Natasha Vladov was to use in emergencies.

"He has escaped," she told him evenly. "The body found in the house belonged to one of the others. We found the van near the train station in Zurich. One of them is injured. There was blood in the van."

He leaned back in his chair and spoke quietly into the receiver. "How many are left?"

"Only three now. McGuire, Ward and the researcher named Sykes," Natasha Vladov answered.

There was a light blinking on his telephone. "Hold on," he told Natasha, and pressed the button.

"Your briefing is in ten minutes, sir," his secretary announced.

"Thank you," he said and spoke into his secure line once again. "Find them."

"And when I do?" Vladov asked.

"Kill Ward," he answered, and disconnected the line.


It was late. Max Rudger was standing in the den of the old farmhouse poking at a log in the fireplace when Richard Ward rounded the corner. "How's the shoulder?" Max asked, without turning around.

"Hurts like a sonofabitch," Ward laughed.

"Drink?"

"You bet," Ward answered, and Max heard the nervousness in his voice, the quivering uncertainty of a man who had put his future in the hands of others. Max handed him a short glass of whiskey and watched him while he drank.

Ward smiled. "Thanks. This will help ... Your

wife was real nice earlier," he commented, as if paying a compliment to a stranger would somehow narrow the distance between them.

Max nodded and sat down. "She's fine, that one."

Richard Ward sat down across from Max and looked at him curiously. "So tell me about this Madison person. What's the deal with her?"

Max grinned. "She thinks you're a piece of shit."

Ward helped himself to another drink. "She told you that?"

Max shook his head. "Didn't have to."

They were silent for a while, until Ward commented thoughtfully, "She lost one of her group tonight. He got it in the chest. A guy named Charlie. You know him?" Max shook his head. "She didn't even look at him twice. She just charged out the door like the fucking cavalry with that 9mm Sig she carries, and when she came back she threatened to kill *me*."

Max chuckled, and Ward went on. "Man, I'm telling you, she's just not human."

Max played with his mustache and took his time about answering. "She's human, all right. Has her dark hours just like the rest of us. She feels, but she deals with it in private. That's the only reason you're still alive, old son."

# — 8 —

A beautiful Swiss morning, bright and beckoning, the air crisp and clean, a fresh layer of unmarked white powder covering fallow fields. Madison took a deep breath and let it out slowly while she gathered up an arm full of split logs and set them by the back door.

"It's a day to love, isn't it, Max?" she said brightly. "A day of absolute beauty. This is the one place that always seems untouched by the rest of the world. Glad you've decided to stay?"

Max brushed off the stump he had been using to

cut firewood and patted it for Madison to sit down. "There's nothin' in Ireland for me anymore. I didn't realize how attached I was to this place till we started talkin' about leavin'." He smiled as she walked towards him, her body dwarfed by his big coat.

"We'll get photographs this afternoon," he told her as she sat on the stump. "It'll take a couple of days for the passports though. I'll take Helen with me to Zurich later and we'll pick up some coats and a change of clothes for the lot of you. You're lookin' pretty pathetic, old girl."

Madison reached to him, wrapped her arm in his. "Thanks, Max."

He pulled the pipe from his pocket and tapped it against his palm, kicking at the dark patch of old tobacco in the snow. "So you think Bradford set up the whole Geneva network thing when he found out Ward met the Russian scientist?"

Madison nodded. "He had Lyle Dresser blackmailed and murdered to draw attention to Geneva. He let Natasha Vladov blow a few agents just to make it look real, then they started setting up Richard Ward. I don't think Bradford counted on us giving Ward a full interrogation. We had enough on him to pull him in without it."

"How high up do you think he goes?"

Madison sighed. "Well, he's been a step ahead of us all the way. His people watching the Lucerne house, the pass with Natasha Vladov in the Square, an enormous amount of money in Ward's account. And last night poor Charlie got it."

Max shook his head. "Christ, Madi, you've really stepped in it this time."

Madison found a cigarette and got a light from Max. "I've got to get to Director Colby. I'll never reach him from here, not with Bradford running interference. I tried to call last night and ended up getting patched through to Fred Nolan who runs the Intelligence section. He told me the Director was ill, had been sent home, doctor's orders. He wanted me to update him on the interrogation with Ward. I didn't tell him anything. I made an excuse and said I'd ring him again or cable."

"You think Nolan could be Bradford?" Max asked.

Madison shrugged. "Anything's possible, I suppose. But the truth is, Max, I can't see any of them doing this. They're all dedicated men."

Max patted her arm gently. "Wish I could help you out, old girl. It's not like the old days though. Can't run around with you any more. I'm goin' to be a father, you know. I've got new responsibilities. I've — "

"A father, Max?" Madison leaped to her feet. "At your age? My God, why didn't you tell me?"

His grin was enormous. "Helen wanted to give you the news right off but I wanted to be the one."

Smiling, Madison said, "You're going to make an absolutely splendid daddy, Max Rudger. The best."

A sudden frown on his big rugged face, he put his forehead to hers. "Aren't you tired of dodgin' bullets, Madi? The kid needs an aunt, you know. Hell, every kid needs a couple of eccentric old aunts. Your luck's bound to run dry one day and I don't want to find myself deliverin' the eulogy at your blasted funeral."

She pulled away from him and walked towards the house. "Do try not to dwell on the negative so much, old man," she said, smiling over her shoulder.

They brushed the snow off their coats and came in the back door. The kitchen was warm and smelled of cookies and fresh bread. Helen was in her apron, standing at the counter chattering at Donna and Richard Ward as if she had known them all her life. She had put her uninvited guests to work, Madison noticed at once. Donna, a white streak of flour across her forehead, was rolling out dough. Richard Ward was pressing a glass into the dough intently, making little circles and laying them on a cookie sheet, then sprinkling sugar on top. It was a mini-production line with Helen as their self-appointed supervisor. Helen peeked over Ward's shoulder and suggested he put the cookies a little closer together, then told Donna the dough would do better if it were a bit thinner. Max and Madison exchanged smiles.

Later, Madison heard Donna telling Ward that spending the morning with Helen was like being held hostage by a menacing version of Donna Reed. They both seemed to find this uproariously funny, but then lapsed into sudden quiet as Madison walked by.

Madison wondered if their alliance was temporary, for she could not see one thing that the two of them might have in common. Perhaps it was Charlie's death that had brought them together. Or perhaps it was because they were strangers in a strange home, or maybe they had simply united against kitchen duty and had chosen Helen as their enemy. Strength in numbers, she thought, walking to the bedroom telephone and dialing Terry.

She used the code they had worked out. If ever anything happened that made Madison believe their telephones were not safe, Madison would say she was in Ireland and Terry would know to find another telephone and ring Max Rudger's number. If Madison wasn't there, Max would know how to reach her.

It took only a few minutes for Terry to call back. She had climbed out of bed a half hour before her alarm was set to go off, thrown on some clothes, jumped in her car and driven to a pay phone in Avon. She was frightened. Madison heard it in her voice and did her best to assure Terry that she was fine. It was simply the telephones Madison was concerned about, she insisted. The agency had a habit of bugging its agents' phones.

But Terry wasn't buying it. "You didn't want the call traced. Why?" she asked.

"Don't be silly, darling. I merely wanted to hear your sweet voice without my employers listening in."

"I love you more than anything, Madison McGuire," Terry said, quietly. "But you're a terrible liar."

Smiling, Madison grabbed a couple of pillows and propped herself up on Max's bed. "Right now I just want to forget the agency and hear every detail of your life."

Terry did not argue. She knew Madison needed to be talked to, talked at, really, about nothing in particular, knew she needed the comfort of knowing

Terry was there, needed to be reminded that she had a life, a happy, full life, outside the Company.

"The rush has started already," Terry said in the voice she used when she was pretending to be bothered. "It's the only time of year I get any respect at all. Half the people are trying to figure out how to cheat the IRS next year and the other half are already in deep shit because they cheated the IRS last year. Oh, I almost forgot. I called Mother today and told her I was a lesbian." There was a grin in her voice.

"Really? Well, that *is* news. How did she take it?"

"She wanted to know why you and I couldn't just be good friends."

"I see," Madison said, smiling. "You know, it really is amazing that she didn't seem to know, isn't it?"

Terry laughed. "My mother has been in a constant state of denial for years now. She's the only person I know who thinks the moon walk was a fake and big time wrestling is real. This is the same woman who sends us cheese logs every year for Christmas, don't forget."

"Yes. I see what you mean," Madison laughed.

"I miss you," Terry said.

"I know."


Max's counterfeiting friend had done an excellent job. The passports, two German, one Swiss, one British, were exactly as Madison had requested.

That afternoon, Donna Sykes and Richard Ward traveled over the German border by train. At Frankfurt am Main, they would show their German passports and board a plane for New York where Old George would pick them up and take them to a place where they would be safe.

Madison flew from Zurich to Heathrow, then used the British passport to board a flight from London direct to Washington, D.C. She bought flat shoes, a briefcase and a tweed skirt, pulled her hair into a tight bun, put on the thick-rimmed glasses, and wore blue contacts to match the passport photo. She might have been anyone's maiden aunt.

At Dulles Airport, she proceeded carefully. If Bradford had people watching incoming flights, and it was certainly logical that he might, they would not be the men from television spy movies with newspapers in front of their faces, dark suits and government issue sunglasses. They would be mothers or pilots, beggars or college students.

Madison watched the people around her, checked out their clothing, their shoes, logging the small things in her memory with the dispassionate ease of a professional. If the watchers were there, Madison had slipped past them. She could detect no one following her, no foot out of step with the crowds, no one loitering, no one rushing to catch up or fall behind when she stopped off for cigarettes, when she bought a magazine and studied the concourse from inside a shop, when she drifted into a lounge and ordered a drink.

Sure at last that she was safe, she rented an

automobile and made a brief phone call before leaving the airport.

Fred Nolan walked into William Ryan's sixth floor office with a mug of coffee in his hand and the look of a man who had not had a full night's sleep in weeks. He settled himself on the edge of Ryan's desk with a sigh. "So what's going on?"

William Ryan was leaning back in his chair, feet propped on the desk, ankles crossed. His light blue shirt was wrinkled, his tie loosened at the collar. The desk was cluttered with papers, a mug half full of old coffee sat near the telephone, and a pen was stuck behind one ear for safe keeping. "I was here at nine o'clock clearing up some paperwork and Jimmy buzzed me from downstairs," Ryan said. "Jimmy's running the switchboard tonight. Madison called in on the agent line, used an emergency code, which threw everyone down there into a panic, and asked to be patched through to the Director. Jimmy didn't know what to do with her so he put her through to me." He sat up and pulled his chair closer to his desk. "Something's wrong, Fred. Madison's spooked. She wouldn't tell me anything."

Nolan frowned. "Any word from her since?"

"Nothing. The call was traced to a phone in the airport, so at least we know she's in town," Ryan answered. "She's been in the field too long. After a while everyone's the enemy. I know what it's like."

Suddenly Nolan had the feeling that Ryan had

just revealed something intimate about his past. He moved to the chair and took a sip of his coffee. "She's failed to send in her reports, she's disappeared with one of our agents, and it looks like she's decided to run Night Trace alone. She shouldn't have been assigned without a controller to keep the operation on track. What was Colby thinking? I swear, Will, sometimes I think he's losing his edge."

Ryan laughed. "The old man is still twice as sharp as me and you put together."

"You think we should pull her in?"

Ryan shook his head. "Night Trace is Mitchell's baby. I don't want to make a move without his approval."

Nolan yawned. "I think we'd better wake the old man."

But the Director of Central Intelligence had already been awakened. Madison McGuire had slipped through the security gates, argued her way past the housekeeper and gotten to Mrs. Colby who, with the sagacity of a seasoned agency wife, understood the urgency and took Madison directly to the Director.

Mitchell Colby was a good ten pounds lighter than when Madison had last seen him. His face was drawn, loose folds of grey skin hung on the wide jowls, but the eyes were sharp and alert with the unspent energy of a person forced into convalescing. He sat quietly — impatiently, Madison judged — and listened to her story.

A blinking light on his private line demanded his attention, and from the look he gave her when he answered, she knew the call was from Langley.

Propped up in his bed, his pajama shirt buttoned to the neck, the receiver cradled on his shoulder, he listened and occasionally mumbled something back grouchily.

Madison glanced around her. Of the bedroom furnishings, everything was wood and dark green colors and very masculine. In one corner was a mahogany desk with a telephone on each end, an old world map in a wood frame hanging above. Two chairs with emerald cushions sat in front of a double window, flanking a magazine rack overflowing with conservative publications. The bed, like the desk, was mahogany, an enormous four-poster with a deep green spread. Madison wondered how long it had been since the Director had shared a bedroom with his wife, for there was no hint of the small, prim, silver-haired woman in this room.

Mitchell Colby replaced the receiver and looked at her in a way she could not define at first, and it crossed her mind in one paranoid instant that he might be considering shooting the messenger who had delivered the bad news. Then she thought that he might have lapsed into a state of complete melancholy. His networks were crumbling around his feet, after all. He must be afraid for his people in the field, afraid of the damage that could result between the CIA and the Intelligence agencies around the world if it got out that there was a mole deep within the Company.

But when he spoke, she realized that she had misjudged the situation. Mitchell Colby was a crusty, shrewd old field man who trusted his instincts above all else and he found it absurd that a mole could have ferreted his way into the high ranks of the Company without being detected. He did not believe her story — that was clear. Not that he thought she was lying. He simply did not believe in Bradford, he was convinced Bradford was no more than a cover story dreamt up by Richard Ward and his Soviet controllers to damage the agency internally.

Madison looked at him in utter amazement. "Richard Ward was nearly killed in the attack on the Lucerne house."

"One of *your* team *was* killed. Not Richard Ward. Remember that. Ward's controllers sent the snipers, not some fictional character called Bradford. Natasha Vladov has been freelancing for them for the last two years. It was a show put on for your benefit to convince you Bradford is real, and keep Ward under your protection until they can decide what to do with him. They're stalling and in the meantime you're doing their job for them, Madison. You're keeping Ward away from our interrogators."

He reached for a tissue and used it to cover his mouth when he coughed. He then folded it carefully and stuffed it into his pajama shirt pocket. Colby believed in conserving everything, Madison remembered. She had once heard that when he took over the agency he had immediately sent a memo out to all departments that all unused sheets of computer paper would be collected and sent to a company to be converted into note pads. A similar memo went to Purchasing, instructing them to cancel all orders for scratch paper.

"If you believe totally, sir," Madison began, "beyond a shadow of a doubt that Bradford does not exist, why then did you not tell your deputies I was here when they called?"

The Director did not like to be questioned. His big hand ran over the fuzz on top of his head, an abrupt movement, tense and annoyed. "You've got seven days to make your case against my boys," he said. "Then I'm pulling Richard Ward in."

"Thank you, sir. I'll need access to Nolan and Ryan's background and case files," she said without emotion, rising from the chair next to his bed.

The Director nodded. "Fair enough. I'll get them to you by messenger, in groups, twenty-four hours at a time. You don't leave the Washington house during these periods and you work alone."

When Madison was nearly through the bedroom door, the Director said, "By the way, no one's been blown since Richard Ward's been off the streets. Think about that."


Madison opened her eyes after a long and much needed sleep, forgetting for a moment where she was. Beirut? Geneva? London? There had been so many safe houses till now, so many patterns of wallpaper, so many shades of paint on strange ceilings.

There was a knocking at the door, quiet, steady, patient, and she knew it was the messenger with the files, the knocking that had awakened her. Only an agency messenger knocks like that, thought Madison, rising quickly and slipping into her clothes. Company messengers always had a particular kind of knock, just as they seemed to have a certain long-suffering tolerance in their tone of voice. They were like watchers in that way, they had spent their lives waiting.

The files signed for and the messenger dispatched with his little clipboard, Madison found the kitchen of the small Washington safe house and started coffee brewing. An anonymous note posted on the wall above the coffee machine instructed the user to put a towel under the coffee maker, as it leaked slightly. Madison smiled at that. Some attentive and, no doubt, distressed agent, in the boredom that so often comes with safe houses, had taken the time to leave the message. She studied the handwriting and guessed the agent had been male.

On a lumpy, yellow sofa, Madison leaned back, sat her coffee and ashtray next to her, propped her feet on a scarred coffee table, and started with Fred Nolan's personnel file.

A Yale graduate, Nolan had gone to work for a Washington think-tank where he remained for eight years. Soon after his marriage he had discovered an interest in Intelligence and applied to the agency. Madison made a note of the date, remembering that Sergi Alexandrovich Novgorok had told Richard Ward that the Soviets had been building their mole for years. The CIA had done the same — bet on young, ambitious recruits and waited for years to reap the benefits. Fifteen years ago would have been about the time Nolan joined the agency. Madison had known him half that time, was even fond of him, but that meant nothing in a business where you never really knew anyone below the surface.

Taking a substantial cut in salary, Nolan had started as a junior analyst attached to the Intelligence section. After a few years and several promotions, he was moved to the screening room where he worked with the top secret video tape that came through the agency, analyzing behavior, actions and reactions of new recruits, doubles, informants, and agents who were not aware they were being filmed during debriefings and interrogations.

In a routine progress report, a superior had written of Fred Nolan: His ability to comprehend and decipher detailed Intelligence has been impressive. He's conscientious and responsible, a real team player.

Nolan's rise to the head of the Intelligence section had been rapid by agency standards. After the former Director had been ousted and Mitchell Colby, a well-known conservative, had taken over and started house cleaning, Nolan was promoted from Senior Analyst and confirmed as Deputy Director.

In a memo unusual in that it was handwritten, Mark Penland from Finance had commented on how spectacularly Nolan had handled the dirty work on an operation called Witness, how he had negotiated reasonable terms with someone named Blitzer and had helped quietly sweep the whole nasty business under the rug.

Madison made a note: *Operation Witness-Blitzer.*

William Ryan's file told the same story of a steady climb to the top of agency hierarchy. Unlike Fred Nolan, however, William Ryan had no college education, had joined the agency at a time when all that was required was an obsessive desire to fight Communism amid the raging Cold War, a time when the line between good and evil was very clearly drawn. From the beginning Ryan seemed destined for the field. He had gone through his Camp Peary training at the head of his class, scored top marks in clandestine entry, recruitment techniques, resisting interrogation, decoding, and weapons handling.

In the field, his performance was outstanding. One of his early assignments had been to Prague. Working under deep cover as a British journalist, Ryan was to assist the Czech underground with its fight against Communist rule. Along with two other American agents, Ryan ran supply lines through Europe into Czechoslovakia, smuggling in printing equipment piece by piece, ink, paper and radios to help the underground with its propaganda campaign. Then, in the summer of 1968, the attempted reforms were crushed. Other Warsaw Pact members moved their tanks in to intervene and the Czech government staged a raid on the underground headquarters. Three members of the group were arrested along with two American agents. Ryan immediately contacted Langley with a plan for a rescue. Langley assisted by setting up escape routes and providing passports for the entire group. In the end, the three members of the underground were arrested at a border crossing, but Ryan got out with the American agents and escaped through Austria.

He was then assigned to Moscow, learned the Soviet system, learned to speak the language fluently, turned more agents around than anyone before him, and worked his way to the head of Moscow station in ten years time. Where Fred Nolan was mild and cooperative and perhaps a bit doughy, Ryan was aggressive, head-strong, persuasive, and likeable. Seemingly quite unlikely to be a mole.

In a memo to the Director of Central Intelligence, the Deputy Director of Operations had written of Ryan soon after his appointment to Moscow: Will's operatives and agents-in-place would run miles for him. He has a way of making people want to please him. He's their big brother, their mother, any damn thing they want him to be. He's got them eating out of his hand and the Intelligence that's coming in is top rate.

Later, Madison found a dated memo in Ryan's own handwriting, expressing his disappointment with Operation Witness and accepting responsibility for its failure since he had recommended agent Frank Blitzer for the operation.

During the next forty-eight hours the messenger returned once with a new load of files, quietly taking back an armful, his face colored from the crisp Washington air, his eyes dutifully avoiding Madison.

She pored over the files, reading about more operations in which Nolan and Ryan had participated, operations with witless names like Verify, Disrupt, Evidence, and Destiny. Once, after reading until her eyes watered and her head hurt, her mind began to wander and she imagined an earnest little man in a bare CIA cubicle dreaming up the labels for operations and patting himself on the back when one seemed particularly inspiring. But, oddly, nowhere did she find an actual case file titled Witness.

A special security clearance from Mitchell Colby and a visit to the records room confirmed Madison's suspicions: The file on Operation Witness was missing and all information on an agent named Frank Blitzer had been deleted from the computer system.

# — 9 —

It was called Lyonsdale, a snowy little town bordering the Adirondacks. Old George had told her to take Highway Twelve past the welcome sign, drive another four miles and turn right on a dirt lane just after the green mailbox. It had taken two passes before Madison had seen the road beneath the snow. With no tire tracks to guide her, if she hadn't spotted the utility pole and the cables running up the lane, she might have missed it a third time. Old George should be assigned to scouting out safe houses for the Company, she thought aimlessly, driving towards the remote mountain hideaway.

The cabin sat three-quarters of a mile off the road, surrounded by evergreens heavy with winter. It was built of stone and log, and on one side the wind had banked the snow nearly as high as the roof. Madison stepped out of the rented four-wheel drive and sank to her knees in white powder.

Donna Sykes and Richard Ward looked like bored housewives. Ward was wearing pajama pants and a flannel shirt, his hair flat in back as if he had just climbed out of bed. Yet he had on his dress shoes. Donna was fully dressed with a worn blue bathrobe over her clothes. She had taken up smoking after a three-year break.

Madison was welcomed like a traveler who brought news from the outside world. Old George had shown up yesterday, they told her, with a television but there was no reception, the radio didn't work, they had nearly worn out their deck of playing cards, and the telephone had been removed. Madison did not bother to tell them it had been taken out at her request.

Like cut-off prisoners, they wanted to know everything before she could even shake the snow off her shoes. What was the news of the day? Would they be home for Christmas? Had Madison called Donna's lover, Pat? Was Richard a hero in the agency for uncovering Bradford?

Madison laughed on her way to the kitchen for something warm to drink. "I'm afraid Bradford is still very much undercover, and you've got a long way to go before you reach hero status, old boy. There is still the questionable handling of your to consider, after all. And, yes, Don, I spoke with Pat. Told her you were fine and that you'd be home soon."

The sink was filled with dirty dishes and Madison guessed that they used every available dish and then washed them all at once. She rinsed out a cup and a pot, found some tea bags and started the water boiling.

Madison sat down in the main room of the small two-bedroom cabin. The ashtrays were full. Empty soda cans littered the end tables and a pair of socks were draped over the back of the couch.

"How do you two live like this? You've only been here a few days. Can't be that bad yet, can it?"

Ward stretched out on the couch, unperturbed, and Donna sneered, "If we'd known we were having company we'd have cleaned up. But shit, we don't even get a goddamned telephone. I feel like I'm being held hostage."

Madison took a sip of tea. "I am sorry about the telephone, Don, truly. But I picked up a few things on the way though. Cigarettes, coffee, a Monopoly board. Even bought a box of chocolates."

Donna looked at Richard Ward. "Hear that, Rich? Chocolate and Monopoly. Jesus, now we have something to live for." She slapped at Ward's feet. "Get off your butt and bring the stuff inside."

Madison watched Ward lumber out the door sulkily in his pajamas. "Don, do you know anything about an operation called Witness? Or someone named Frank Blitzer?"

Donna ran a hand through her silver hair and crinkled her forehead. "Witness," she repeated quietly. Her blue eyes gave a little sparkle, and

Madison thought that perhaps the opportunity to use her mind for something other than gin rummy had breathed new life into her.

"I remember Witness and Blitzer too," she answered at last. "It started six months before I was kicked out. It was one of the schoolboys' operations."

"The schoolboys?" Madison asked.

"The little piss-ants Colby calls deputies." She paused and thought about that. "Except Ryan maybe. He doesn't really fit into the piss-ant category. Ryan's okay."

Richard Ward came in shivering. "We've got food, eggnog, games and cheap paperbacks. And last but not least — " He withdrew two bottles from the bag triumphantly. "She brought us booze. God, this is great."

The small things, Madison knew, bring tremendous pleasure when one has been forced underground.

"Do you remember any of the operational details?" she asked, looking back at Donna.

Richard Ward appeared again, this time with three glasses. "What'll it be, scotch or bourbon?"

Donna ordered bourbon and Coke, then began in her storytelling voice, "Witness started as a Moscow station operation." Madison lit a cigarette, knowing how Donna loved to draw out a story.

"Blitzer," Donna resumed, "was working Moscow at the time. He cabled that he had a Head Red in the Kremlin ready to come around. Code name Leo. Everyone knew something big was happening. There was real excitement in the air." She paused and shook her head. "God, I really miss those days. You know how it is when there's a big operation on.

Even with compartmentalization you can't keep it quiet. There's code clerks, interpreters, typists, Finance to approve payments, Records to put the stuff somewhere, and believe me there was a lot of stuff coming in, twice a week by diplomatic bag and in the code rooms too. The Company was buzzing."

Wanting to keep Donna on track, Madison interrupted as delicately as possible. "And the Intelligence itself, exciting stuff too, was it, Don?"

Donna nodded enthusiastically. "Mostly street level stuff at first. Leo was playing with us, I think, testing the water. But then he started sending in copies of reports on things like Soviet sentiment towards the Afghanistan problem, failure of a totalitarian system, propaganda campaigns to discourage any sign of independence in the Baltic states. The kind of stuff no Russian would turn over if he wasn't for real. I was instructed to handle it myself and keep the clerks away from it," she added proudly.

At the risk of breaking the spell, Madison cut in. "Who gave you the order?"

Donna shrugged. "One of the schoolboys. Nolan, I think, maybe Mark Penland from Finance . . . Anyway, after a couple of months Leo decided he was selling out too cheap, I guess. He wanted more money, lots of it, thirty thousand francs a month into a Swiss account, which verified in a way that Leo was at the top. He had to have mobility, a lot of freedom or he could have never gotten to the money. Then he decided he wanted assurances, assurances Frank Blitzer couldn't give him. He wanted to know who the top man was running the operation." She turned down the corners of her mouth sympathetically. "You know, I think the guy just wanted to feel important."

Madison nodded. Agents-in-place the world over, no matter how high or low in rank, believed they were providing the Company with the most vital information it had ever received, believed their Intelligence was significant above all else and they wanted to be treated importantly. Sometimes it meant only a token acknowledgement or a few extra dollars. Sometimes a clandestine meeting with a Station Chief would assure them, sometimes it took more.

"And you got all this from the files?" Madison asked.

Donna added a bit more bourbon to her glass. "Maybe I read between the lines a little. I mean, I never actually discussed it with the schoolboys."

"So who took over the operation at that point, after Leo became dissatisfied with Blitzer?"

"Leo said he wanted a signal, some message from the top. So, as a show of support the Company sent Nolan, Ryan and Penland to Moscow for some big gathering at the embassy. Of course, they never met Leo because the KGB was all over them as soon as they arrived, but sending them was the message Leo wanted. After that Frank Blitzer continued as the legman. Then one day the axe fell and I got a pink slip."

Madison thought about that for a moment, then leaned forward and said mildly, "Let me be sure I follow, Don. You're Head of Records, the only one in the department cleared for Witness. The operation's at its peak. Leo's satisfied again and sending in superb Intelligence. You're filing the stuff, color-coding it and whatever else you did, cross-referencing, I suppose. Then one day you find yourself unemployed?"

Donna shook her head. "The operation *wasn't* at its peak. It had dried up. Just stopped suddenly. Not a piece of paperwork coming through. Then Frank Blitzer was hauled in and handed over to the interrogators. Rumors were he'd sold out to the Russians. Next, I got the boot and a dozen or so others from code clerks to analysts got early retirement and full pensions."

"What happened to Blitzer then? Did you hear?" Madison asked.

"He got a new name. Harris, I think. Someone said he went to Denver."

"And what was the official reason for your dismissal?" Madison inquired gently, trying not to sound like an interrogator and knowing also that this was a sensitive spot with Donna.

Donna took a drink and spoke with a bitter narrowing of her blue eyes. "Insecure lifestyle or something equally inane. They decided I was a security risk. They knew all along I was a lesbian. But they don't implement policies like that till it suits their purpose. They file it, squirrel it away, protect it like a secret treasure till they need it. They'll do the same to you, Madison, as soon as you fall out of favor with the court."

But Madison did not want to look that far ahead. "Why do you think they suddenly wanted you out?" she asked, carefully. "Was there one thing you could point to? Was it just anyone who knew about Witness that got sacked?"

Donna sank back into her chair, her chin pressed

towards her chest. She was looking down with a disheartened expression into the drink she held in her small hands, and Madison knew she had lost her. If Donna had heard the question at all, she had decided not to respond.

The reception area was small, the floor covered with a tan level-loop one might find in a doctor's office. Christmas music poured through a ceiling speaker. Outside, Denver already had its white Christmas. The streets were full of shoppers and snow and grumblings of a football team that could never seem to win the big ones.

He stepped into the lobby, a slightly heavy-set man in a blue suit, with a hawkish nose and thin arched brows set on a thick ridge over his eyes. The eyes themselves were clever and almond-shaped with little gold flecks mixed in the brown. He carried a note in his hand that the lobby receptionist had taken to him and he consulted it before he spoke.

"Ms. McGuire? I'm Frank Harris," he said, extending one huge hand. "Come in." He turned on the way into his office and smiled, and for the first time Madison noticed the slight limp. "Some day, huh? Probably a rerun of last year. It'll snow from now till spring. Always snows here when you don't really need it."

Two plaques hung behind his desk, both black with gold letters; one announcing the company's contributions to the YMCA, the second from the Chamber of Commerce. A dreadful color poster tacked to the side wall vividly illustrated the dangers of going without enough automobile insurance to cover injured passengers in an accident.

He watched her eyes sweep the walls, and chuckled knowingly. "It is an awful poster, I know. Sells a hell of a lot of insurance though. What can I do for you, Ms. McGuire? My secretary said you're looking for donations for — "

"I'm afraid I misled your secretary, Mr. Blitzer. Perhaps we could have lunch and talk a bit."

His eyes locked on her for a moment. Without a word he stood and closed the office door. "I thought the name was familiar," he announced coldly, sitting back down behind his desk. "The least you could do is use a work name if you have to come here. It's been tough enough to build a life on the outside."

Madison nodded. "I'm sorry. It never occurred to me. I've used so many names I would have thought McGuire would be fresh again by now." She smiled but received no smile in return.

"What do you want?" he asked, looking to his desk, moving a few stacks of paper around awkwardly.

"I really do think it better that we talk somewhere else."


"Why have you come?" he asked, after they had parked the car and started the walk around Mile High Stadium.

"What can you tell me about Witness? About Leo?" Madison asked.

He stopped. "Jesus, not this again. I went through five days and nights of hell with the same questions after I got back from Moscow. Thought the Company would have gotten a big enough piece of me by now. Is this why they've sent you? I suppose someone's waiting to sweat me."

Madison offered him a cigarette, and lit one for herself when he didn't accept. "I'm alone."

He started walking again, taking long uneven strides, keeping a step or two ahead. "Leo was going to tell you about a mole in the Company, wasn't he?" she asked, raising her voice enough so he could hear. He didn't stop. He didn't respond. "A mole, Frank, a Soviet mole. Is that when Witness came apart?"

He spun around, his face red with cold or anger, Madison was not sure which. Until he spoke. "Read the fucking file."

"I came to hear your side of the story."

At this, Frank Harris, formally Frank Blitzer of Moscow station, laughed heartily and pulled a silver flask from the inside pocket of his long coat and took a drink. "I told the interrogators my side already but they weren't listening."

"Please, just once more," Madison insisted quietly.

He sighed and shrugged. "Leo sent me a message, said things were heating up and he was getting worried. He hinted at knowing the identity of a Soviet deep penetration agent in the CIA. I was to meet him that Saturday at the park in the *Oktyabrsky* district. We'd only had one meeting face to face. It was usually dead drops and couriers. I should have known then that something was wrong. But I had stars in my eyes, I guess."

"And up to that point Leo had never mentioned a mole?"

"Not a word." He took another drink and passed the flask to Madison, who took it out of politeness.

"So what happened then?"

He limped ahead of her, looking straight ahead as he spoke, so that Madison had to strain to hear. "I shed my western clothes, did my best to look the part of a half-starved Russian, and showed up for the meeting. It was in the park at night. We were supposed to meet at the statue of Lenin on the east end. Leo was late. After ten minutes I started going through the backup procedures. We had worked it out so if he didn't show I would stop by a certain restaurant. They would advertise this special for the day outside, Tabaka chicken and pomegranate sauce, and I would know Leo was okay and for the next three days we would try the meeting again, same place, same time. I had just gotten back to downtown Moscow and walked past the restaurant when all hell broke loose. The next thing I knew, about five black Volgas pulled up and guys with guns were piling out, shouting like crazy for me to stop. They seemed surprised when I ran. They didn't react right away. I think the bastards really expected me to just stand there and let them haul me away. The average Russian has been so defeated and so terrified for so long, I don't think they even consider escape as an option. But I ran like hell. I took a bullet in my leg and I still ran faster than I ever ran in my life. I made it to a friend's apartment and stayed there until I could get word to the agency. It was about twenty-four hours later someone picked me up and got me out."

They had almost circled the stadium once, Frank's limp becoming more pronounced, Madison's face stinging from the bitter winter wind. This time Madison accepted the flask gratefully.

"Tell me about the debriefing," she said, taking a sip and recapping his bottle.

"The bastards kept me awake for God knows how long. I've never been through a debriefing like that in my life. I told them about Leo, about our drop sites, I even broke my own rules and turned over the names of my couriers ... Hell, I told them everything I could think of and whatever else I could make up to get them to leave me the hell alone. But, like I said, they weren't listening. I didn't understand until later what they were after."

Madison wanted to ask what he meant, but she sensed it would be better to play along. On a hunch, she asked, "Who told you?"

"My old pal Will."

"I assume you mean Will Ryan. You were friends?"

He stopped to massage his calf briefly, and nodded. "Will helped me cut my teeth in Moscow. Showed me the ropes. The best boss I ever had and one of the best friends."

"What did he say exactly? You remember?"

"He came to see me after the debriefing," Frank answered. "I knew something was wrong when I saw his face. He told me the Company thought I'd sold out to the Russians. He never believed it but there was nothing he could do to help me. He said the whole Witness operation was a Soviet scam. They had planted Leo and used me to track our agents and shut down courier lines. They were keeping track of all the drop sites I set up and all the couriers that picked up the messages from Leo. The

Company interrogators thought I'd known all along and I was playing both sides. One side for glory, I suppose, one side for money. Leo used the story about the mole to reel me in, I guess. He knew I'd never risk meeting him unless it was big." He shook his head. "I suppose the network was rolled up soon after that."

"Did anyone else come to see you after the debriefing, Frank?"

He nodded. "Fred Nolan, the little bald bastard. Treated me like scum. Said he was sorry they hadn't been able to prove their case against me. Wanted to know how I beat the box, then he wanted to know what it would take to keep me quiet. I told him all I wanted was the pension I was owed and to be left alone."

He stopped suddenly and touched Madison's arm. "Do you know anything about my network? The couriers? Did they get out?"

"I don't know. I'm sorry," she answered, moved by his pain.

He walked ahead of her again. "The hopeless games of the Cold War," he muttered quietly, pulling out his silver flask. "And me as their pawn . . . Checkmate."

Madison left Denver without telling Frank Blitzer that there really was a mole in the agency, or that he had escaped the KGB that night in Moscow only because they had wanted him to escape, only because Bradford had to bring him home and discredit him completely to save himself.

# — 10 —

The Soviet Commercial Attache, Dmitri Segeyevich Krasavchenko, stood in the corridor smiling and nodding at the junior staff as they left their desks for the evening and filed out.

"Ah, Alexsi, how is your family?" he asked, smiling at one of the code clerks as he walked through the security scanners for the evening shift. "I hear you will be going home soon."

"Yes, my application has been approved. I leave

next week. It has been almost a year since I have seen them."

Dmitri smiled and patted him affectionately as he passed. "We will miss you, my friend."

He stepped back into his office and picked up the secure telephone line blinking on his desk.

"Hello, Dmitri Segeyevich." The stern voice belonged to his chief controller in Moscow. "I have been instructed to begin damage control procedures on the Bradford line."

"He assures me the situation is under control," Dmitri answered patiently. "This is not the time for extreme measures. We can wait out the storm."

"Did he also tell you that he has been using Natasha Vladov? That, my friend, *is* an extreme measure. He is frightened and that frightens us."

"He knows bringing Vladov in was a mistake," Dmitri answered. "He is going to call her off. The operation is still salvageable. After all, our friends believe they have found their mole. The agency intends to quietly pursue the case against Richard Ward."

"Then why have they not yet begun? If they are so convinced, what are they waiting for? I am sorry, Dmitri, but have my orders also. We have an opportunity to inflict some external damage. I admit a destabilization campaign is not as fruitful as running a double, but it is at least something to walk away with. We have authorized our European agents to begin leaking the information. No names, of course, only the fact that we have run a successful infiltration operation against the

Americans for years. Soon no one will want to trade secrets with Langley."

"And what becomes of Bradford?" Dmitri asked.

"He is a hero here. He knows this. He could have a good life."

Minutes later, Dmitri Segeyevich Krasavchenko instructed his driver to drop him at the corner of Kemp Street. He stepped into the cold drizzle and walked back half a block towards the house, his strides long and even, shoulders held straight, head tilted back. He was a large man, overweight with wavy grey-brown hair and a thick mustache. A car passed and Dmitri turned his head away from the bright lights as he started up the sidewalk.

He paused at the front door and turned to look at the house across the street. Loud music was playing, shaded figures with drinks in their hands danced. Dmitri Segeyevich smiled. He liked the neighborhood, liked the activity, liked the college students who moved in and out, scarcely noticing him at all.

Moments later Madison McGuire was knocking on the door of the house across the street. She too had heard the music and seen the party inside.

A young man answered the door and smiled. A cloud of pot smoke billowed out behind him. "I'm having car trouble," Madison explained. "I wonder if I might use your telephone and wait inside for my ride." She pointed to the bag she was carrying. "I'm a photographer. I'm afraid the rain will damage my equipment."

He nodded. "No problem. There's a phone upstairs. It's kind of noisy down here. Want a drink or something?"

136

Madison smiled. "No thanks."

"Whatever," he shrugged and went back to his party, forgetting her almost as soon as she disappeared.

Moments later Madison had found an empty bedroom with a view of the house across the street. She removed the camera from her bag, snapped the long lens into place, cut the lights, raised the window and waited.

When she pressed the shutter release for the first time, she got several shots of Krasavchenko leaving the house. Minutes later the Deputy Director of Operations for the Central Intelligence Agency, William Ryan, stepped out into the drizzle. Madison held the shutter and let the auto-winder do its job until the roll was finished.

The heavy drapes had been closed and the only light in the Director's room was coming from a single reading lamp on his desk. It cast a bright light on the pages in front of him, throwing dark contrasting shadows across his face and hands. Madison knew the housekeeper had alerted him to her visit, knew he had heard her step through the half opened door. Still, he did not look up for quite some time.

"Good to see you up and around, sir," Madison commented cautiously, testing his mood, knowing his confinement had made him more irritable than usual.

He turned slowly and removed his gold-rimmed reading glasses. "How was Denver?" he asked dryly.

Madison smiled and held up her index finger, moving it left to right like a school teacher about to deliver a lesson. "You've had me followed, have you?"

The Director puckered his lips disapprovingly and narrowed his eyes. "I was curious as to why you hadn't been in touch. Advise me of your travel plans from here on, McGuire. You're not running this operation alone."

Madison moved closer and dropped a manila envelope under the shaft of light on the Director's desk. "Perhaps you'll forgive me my indiscretions when you see these."

He took the envelope with him to the window and pulled open the drapes. Madison watched his back as he withdrew the first photograph, then quickly went through the others.

"Where did you get these?" he asked, calmly. Too calmly, Madison thought.

"I took them last night. It's Dmitri Segeyevich Krasavchenko, the Soviet Commercial Attache. He and Ryan met last night. The meeting lasted approximately forty-five minutes. My report is in the envelope."

He swung around with surprising energy, pointing the photographs at her as if they were a weapon. "Goddammit, McGuire, you know better than to ever get close to a safe house without authorization."

"This isn't the safe house, sir. It's number five-seventeen Kemp Street. I followed Krasavchenko there from the embassy."

"I know where it is," he barked. "I knew about

the meeting. Jesus, don't you realize you might have gotten in the way of an important operation?"

Madison's mind was churning. "This is the man the Russian scientist said was running Bradford. *Bradford's* controller. I'm afraid I don't understand the problem. I've just given you proof that your Head of Operations is ..."

"He's ours, dammit," the Director exclaimed angrily, and Madison looked at him blankly. "Dmitri Krasavchenko is ours. He's working for us. Will Ryan's been running him since he came to Washington. Your time is up, Madison. Give me Richard Ward and take some time off."

They had brought him to this place twenty-four hours ago, a dacha somewhere just outside Moscow, for the sounds of traffic had only just disappeared completely when they pulled onto the dirt road and untied his blindfold. Suddenly Dan Wright found himself treated to special privileges — a country house, cupboards stocked with food that had never been available in the city, freedom to move about, even short walks with his KGB guard.

He was tired and underweight, and in his dreams he still saw the doctor's face and felt the needle as it slipped under the skin, heard the muffled voices of his interrogators, heard his own screams.

He looked out the window and saw his babysitters outside smoking, talking, occasionally glancing towards the road. He had seen men wait before and they were waiting for something big, he knew. He felt the impermanence of his situation, felt the tension in his babysitters, but no one told him anything. No one offered to ease his mind. This was a place of questions, not answers.

London's Hungerford Bridge at night, a place where lovers huddled together against the damp, where couples kissed and planned their escape, a place right out of an old black and white movie, so still, so wintry, so full of whispers.

He was American, based for many years in Britain; she was Russian; they were old adversaries hesitant to trust. She had sent the message, proposed the meeting. They faced each other from opposite ends of the bridge, both with their hands plunged into the pockets of their raincoats.

"It's all a game, you know," she said when they had come together. "And sometimes you must sacrifice one game piece to gain another. A red checker for a black one, a knight for a knight."

The American agent looked at her curiously. She smiled. "Send the message to your Director and only your Director. He will understand."

In a hotel on the outskirts of Washington, Madison sat for a while in the dressing table chair, too tired for the long drive home. She thought of calling Terry, but Terry would know something was wrong and Madison would hear the concern. She wanted none of it, wanted only to sit in that dark unsympathetic room alone, for there is no one more inconsolable than an agent suddenly faced with failure.

In the drawers she found only a bible and a week-old Cable Guide for reading. On the bed table there was hotel stationery and a beige pen with the hotel name scrolled in orange on the side. Madison studied it aimlessly for a while before dialing room service. She had not planned on having to endure leisure time.


He was a small man, bearded, dark suit, brisk walk. Fred Nolan, William Ryan and Senior Analyst Warren Moss first saw him through the glass office walking towards them importantly, shoulders held very straight.

"Looks like Taylor's got something on his mind," Ryan observed.

"I wish to hell British Intel would send someone else. I always get the feeling Taylor's laughing at me," said Warren Moss seriously, which drew a chuckle from the others.

Ryan opened the office door and smiled. "How are you, Lawrence? Good to see you again."

"Ah, William my boy, glad you could be here. Hello Fred, Warren." Taylor slung his long overcoat over the back of a chair and straightened his tie. His shirt was light blue, expensive, monogrammed at the pocket. A gold watch peeked out from under one cuff. "Shall we?" he asked, like a man who was accustomed to taking control of meetings. He sat down and linked his wiry little hands together, placing them on the conference table.

"What's on your mind, Lawrence?" Nolan asked. "Something we can help you with?"

"Actually we've had some rather disturbing news," Taylor began, looking at his fingernails. "Frankly, we're a bit muddled up over it. Thought you might want to clarify. We have information to suggest you've had a double agent in your midst, that you've known about that agent and you chose to keep it hidden from British Intelligence. How would you respond to that, please?" he asked like a reporter sniffing out a hot story.

Nolan and Ryan exchanged a quick glance. Moss played with the handle of his coffee cup without looking up, for Warren Moss knew his own limits, knew he was inexperienced when it came to this type of confrontation.

"We have no formal agreement on these matters, of course," Taylor continued delicately. "But we believed it was mutually understood that we share information when it affects our security. You must tell us if we've been compromised in any way."

"Check your sources, Lawrence," Nolan answered. "This is news to us."

"Our sources are *quite* reliable." Taylor had obviously taken offense at the suggestion. "And until we feel certain you have our best interests in mind as well as your own, I'm afraid we'll be unable to pass anything your way."

Moss looked up through heavy eyebrows. Nolan said, "We have joint operations underway, Lawrence. You can't pull out."

"It's the Americans who have pulled out, not the British."

William Ryan held up a hand and smiled diplomatically. "All right. We're all friends here. The fact is, Lawrence, we had a problem but it's under control now."

"Oh dear, shades of Kim Philby — on your side this time, is it?" Taylor suggested. "How much china has been broken?"

Ryan gave Moss a stiff nod. "The leak was relatively low level," Moss answered. "The agent hasn't had access to anything that could damage our joint relations. Plus, we've had him off the street for a couple of weeks now."

They watched Taylor gather his coat in his arms and disengage himself gracefully from the office, watched him walk down the corridor seriously, a soldier going home with news of the front.

"Shades of Kim Philby," Moss muttered absurdly. "Don't they just wish. The Brits have been waiting for something like this to throw up to us, and this is just the beginning. The liaison from Israeli Intelligence wants to see us this afternoon."

Ryan sighed. "It's gonna be a long day."


There were two of them, serious and well dressed, one male, one female. They had come quietly, the sound of their tires masked by the wind cracking frozen tree branches.

The woman produced an identification badge ceremoniously. Her eyes darted over Donna Sykes' shoulder as she spoke. "We've come to take you back for your debriefing."

They stepped into the cabin just as Richard Ward was coming out of the kitchen, drying his hands on a dish towel.

"Keep your hands where we can see them," the woman ordered.

Jolted by their sudden appearance, Richard Ward let the towel fall and raised his hands.

Donna looked at the agents in utter disbelief. "Oh, yeah, better get those guns out. A dish towel can be a dangerous weapon in the hands of a professional."

"Stay out of the way, Ms. Sykes." It was the male agent who spoke this time. "You're not involved in this."

Donna watched as the agents secured Ward's wrists behind his back, saw his eyes pass over her, frightened and embarrassed like those of a man on his way to a hanging.

The cabin door opened. The woman stepped out first. And then Richard Ward heard the sudden burst of gunfire from somewhere in the trees. The agent in front of him was down, the one behind him had hit the ground, weapon drawn, and Donna Sykes never took a step from the cabin.

Richard Ward raced toward the agent's brown sedan, zigzagging, hurling himself towards the vehicle for protection, rolling, trying desperately to regain some balance with his hands bound behind his back. The bullets followed him, digging up the snow in great explosions of white. He leaned against one of the tires, sweat pouring from his hairline, partially blinding him as he bent to look around the car towards the trees.

He looked to the cabin. The woman had been killed. The male agent was on his stomach, firing towards the trees. "Cut me loose or I'm a dead man," Ward yelled.

The agent scooted towards him on his stomach, drawing the sniper fire. He was only a few yards from the car when Ward heard his scream, saw the pain in his face. He stopped moving.

Then the gunfire ceased as abruptly as it had begun and Ward knew they must be coming for him. To sit there, wrists tied and helpless, was to die. He struggled to his knees and tried to pull his hands free.

It was then that she stepped around the vehicle, the Mac-10 in her hands, and he knew her immediately. He had seen her once before, thousands of miles away in a cobbled square — a lifetime ago it seemed to him now. Her eyes were dark and wild, and he saw them narrow slightly as she squeezed the trigger.

# — 11 —

The houses were scattered, spread out along the coastline like sentries forbidding unauthorized passage. Most of them were large summer homes, most of them empty. Only a few people had remained to see the hurricane months of fall and the sunless days of winter. Hotels sprang out of the landscape here and there as one moved closer towards the more populated areas of Rodanthe Island and Cape Hatteras. The sand rose up in mounds like snow banks; weeds, brown from winter, grew through the tops. It seemed to Madison like a very long time since she had been home.

The house was cluttered with Terry's things. An extra pair of shoes next to the front door, jeans slung over a chair, a half-empty coffee mug on the dining room table next to a stack of legal papers. She had seen Terry have her coffee at that table so many times while clearing up a last bit of paperwork before going to the office ... and then she'd check her watch and hurry out the door, forgetting both her coffee and her papers.

A small, full pine tree stood in the corner of the living room, undecorated, waiting for Madison's return. Around it were several cardboard boxes marked CHRISTMAS where Terry had retrieved last year's decorations. Under it, Stray Cat, the straggly white feline that had adopted them, drank water from the stand and stretched indifferently.

Madison picked her up and carried her to the couch. "Mad at me for leaving you again, is that it?" she asked, scratching the scruffy chin affectionately. Stray Cat quickly put aside her resentments and curled up in Madison's lap, purring happily.

Madison was in the kitchen when she heard the key in the latch. She knew that Terry would not know she was there, had not seen the car in the garage, because for some inexplicable reason Terry hated that garage. Madison had tried to impress upon her the benefits of having it there. She had told her it was more secure, told her it would protect her car from the salt air. But Terry was stubborn about small things, as people sometimes are who have less control over the big things in their lives.

"Welcome home," Madison said, meeting her at the door.

Wordlessly, Terry wrapped her arms around Madison and held her there for quite some time.

"Did you see the tree?" she finally asked, in a diversionary tactic to draw away Madison's attention from her tears. They no longer spoke of Terry's fears that Madison might not one day return from an assignment.

"It's lovely. Cut it yourself?"

Terry laughed and punched Madison's arm playfully. "Sure. Had to get out the old chain saw, but hey, I was feeling butch and it *is* almost Christmas."

Madison smiled. "Shall we decorate tonight then?"

Terry linked her arm in Madison's and led her to the couch. "How long?" she asked. It was always the first question, the one Madison dreaded the most.

"You have me for a while, I think."

"Can you tell me anything?" Terry asked.

"Well, let's see. Max and Helen seem very happy. I told you on the phone that she's pregnant. Looks wonderful. I was in Denver for a day. It was snowing. That's about it, really. A most unspectacular assignment."

Terry put her head in Madison's lap and reached up to touch her cheek, smiling. "You're a liar, Madison McGuire."

They decorated the Christmas tree, they drank apple cider and had a gas fire in the fireplace. They made love in the living room, then slept in, made breakfast and ate it with the Christmas tree lights burning. They took a walk on the beach and talked about Terry's tax law practice, which was fighting for its life and losing the battle. They drove into Ocracoke and took the ferry to Cedar Island for lunch. They stopped in Cape Hatteras and bought an oil painting of the lighthouse, and hung it over the fireplace in their house.

And then the call came. Mitchell Colby. Terry sat quietly, listening, hating him for the intrusion.

Donna Sykes had gone through her debriefing with no trouble and was on her way home, he told Madison. But Richard Ward never made it back to Langley.

"I have to go," she told Terry when she hung up. "They're sending a chopper. I'm sorry."

"Mitchell," William Ryan exclaimed, when his office door opened and the Director stuck his head in. "You're not supposed to be up so soon."

"I can sit around here as well as I can sit at home. How's your schedule? I'd like to see you, Fred and Warren in my office."

Ryan nodded agreeably. "I'll buzz them. How's a half hour sound?"

The Director was at his desk reading over the field reports on Richard Ward when they arrived. "Come in, boys. Coffee?"

The Director poured four cups from the old pot behind his desk and handed three across the desk. "Give me your thoughts on this thing with Ward," he said, looking over his cup.

"We have to assume it was the Soviets," Nolan answered. "They wouldn't want us to know how they were running him or what kind of Intelligence they ended up with."

"How the hell did they find him?" The Director did not hide his anger well. "Can one of you tell me that?"

Warren Moss shrugged. "He was cut off up there. Madison saw to that. No telephone, no radio, miles from the closest neighbor and up to his ass in snow with no vehicle. There's no way he could have told anyone where he was. Donna Sykes confirmed that. She was with him twenty-four hours a day."

Mitchell Colby looked at the report. "Says here there was only one of them. The tracks were female. No one in town noticed any strangers passing through, and Sykes was cowering in the bedroom."

"The Bureau is still looking for anything that might help identify the killer. No luck yet," Nolan said.

"I agree with Fred," Ryan said. "They were trying to keep him quiet. I mean they've run the guy for God knows how long and they don't want us to know their techniques."

Warren Moss cleared his throat and added thoughtfully, "Donna Sykes said something interesting in the debriefing. She said she had studied Richard Ward carefully and come to the conclusion that he just wasn't smart enough to be a double agent."

On the monitor near his desk, Mitchell Colby watched their backs as they left his office. He watched them walk down the seventh floor corridor, watched Ryan exchange friendly words with the guards at the check point, watched Nolan pass without speaking, watched Moss lumber down the corridor, alone.


The Director of Central Intelligence had few real facial expressions, and even when he allowed himself those rare kindnesses — offering coffee or calling you by your first name — his expression might be one of aggravation. But today Madison could see in him a deep concern. There was a despondency about Mitchell Colby, like a man who had just suffered intolerable defeat or had his heart broken in love.

He offered his hand, a rare and intimate gesture, something he had not done since they had first met. "My deputies think Ward was killed by a Soviet agent. What do you think?"

"You already know what I think, sir. Richard Ward was not your mole. I think Bradford panicked when he found out Ward was coming in to the interrogators. It's his first big mistake. We could have hung Ward with the evidence we had."

"Yes," the Director agreed quietly. "That's what I was thinking." He opened his desk drawer and withdrew a sheet of paper. "This came from one of our operatives in England. A Soviet agent gave him the message."

" 'A knight for a knight,' " Madison said quietly, reading the message. "This proves Rich Ward wasn't our man. The Soviets are telling us they want

Bradford. They're willing to make an exchange." She looked at the Director hopefully. "Does this mean Dan Wright is alive?"

The Director nodded. "It's got to be Wright."

"And you'd be willing to make an exchange? Let Bradford off that easy?"

"Providing there is absolutely no publicity, yes," Colby answered. "I'd give them their agent to protect this agency. What are your feelings?"

"Dan Wright is a good friend, Mr. Colby. I'm afraid I can't be totally objective. But if it were up to me, I'd say yes."

"Well, the Soviets aren't going to blow their own agent, not yet anyway. It's still up to us to find him before any deals can be made."

Madison thought about that. "How many others have been involved with the running of Dmitri Krasavchenko?"

"Fred Nolan has met with him on several occasions, Mark Penland from Finance and Warren Moss once or twice and then there was Will," the Director answered. Then he added quietly, "I heard someone ask once, how do you spy on a spy? I hoped I'd never have to figure it out."

"I assume the sessions with Krasavchenko have been recorded."

Colby nodded. "I'll have the tapes sent to you at the old safe house. It's hardly used anymore."

At the door, Madison turned and smiled. "By the way, sir, it's good to see you up and around."

The Director might not have heard. "Use my private elevator, please," he said distractedly. "I don't want anyone to know you're back just yet. I'll have transportation waiting for you downstairs."

Madison stopped in the outer office and made a phone call. "Looks like I'll be home for Christmas after all," she told Terry. "Thought you'd want to know. Should be wrapping it up here in a day or so. Everything all right at home?"

"It's looking up. I think I have a new client," Terry answered cheerfully. "She called this morning and we're meeting later. A referral."

Madison smiled. "You're very good, you know. I imagine you'll be getting more and more of those. Good luck, darling. I'll see you soon."

"Madison."

"Yes?"

"I really miss you when you're away. I just wanted you to know that."

A run-down safe house in a run-down neighborhood. A leaky coffee pot and a rust-stained bathtub. Fresh linens had been installed by one of the unseen custodians who care for Company houses, who come like shadows when the houses are empty, who grocery shop and dust shelves, who fill medicine cabinets with shaving cream and razors, toothbrushes and shampoo and try half-heartedly to anticipate the other needs of agents.

The pantry was full of canned spaghetti and soups. The refrigerator contained two six-packs of beer and a package of pimento loaf that Madison might have eaten had she been starving. Deciding to skip dinner, she made coffee and read a day-old newspaper while she waited for the messenger with the tapes.

And after the delivery was made, Madison sat in the small living room, headphones on, watching the tape reels spin slowly clockwise while she listened to the recorded sessions with Dmitri Krasavchenko. Sometimes Fred Nolan was the inquisitor, sometimes Ryan, and twice she heard Penland and Warren Moss. She heard Krasavchenko questioned courteously, heard his deep, polished voice answer with so little restraint that he might have been reading a shopping list rather than betraying his country. In one meeting Ryan calmed Krasavchenko's professed fears of exposure, in another Penland promised payments of a certain amount. Nolan collected diplomatic gossip and operational data, and Warren Moss pleaded for Intelligence more technical in nature. But nowhere on the tapes was there one hint of Bradford.

"About the system in the Kemp Street house," Madison said to the Director after hours of listening to the tapes. "I assume it's voice activated."

"Yes," the Director answered. "But I'm looking at the specs right now. It's an old system, Madison. It's controlled from inside the house."

"So Bradford could have turned it on or off whenever it was convenient."

"I'm afraid so," Colby answered. "We're going to have to draw him out. It's the only way."


Armed with an identification badge that allowed her access to all floors of the Central Intelligence Agency, Madison McGuire first stopped by the third floor and said hello to Senior Analyst Warren Moss.

154

She then made her way upstairs and dropped in on Mark Penland, saying she had been waiting to be reimbursed for expenses incurred in Switzerland and would appreciate it very much if he could use his influence to hurry the payment along. Next came Fred Nolan's sixth floor office where she found Ryan and Nolan together.

"Madison," Nolan said, rising from his chair. "Thought you got sent home for the holidays. Come on in. We're just talking."

"I can't stay. Just thought I'd pop in and say hello. The old man wants to see me. Something about Richard Ward."

Nolan and Ryan exchanged glances. "Did he say what?" Nolan asked.

Madison shrugged. "I don't know, the shooting I suppose."


Mitchell Colby was waiting for her in his office. "I made the rounds, sir. They all know you suspect something."

Colby nodded. "Now we wait for Bradford to get spooked. You'd better get set up. It shouldn't take long."

Madison started out of the building, but something stopped her, something Terry had said on the telephone earlier that registered in her subconscious. *A new client.*

Suddenly, she was trembling. Her legs felt weak as she stepped off the elevator and rushed to a telephone on a nearby desk. I've been under too much pressure, she thought, I'm overreacting.

She pressed in the number and stood paralyzed when she heard the receiver lift and no answer. "Terry?" she asked, and then Madison McGuire heard the words that sent a wave of pure terror surging through her.

"I've been waiting for your call, Madison." The voice was low, Slavic, female. "You have been in my way for weeks. It is time we meet face to face. Come alone and your Terry may live through the night."

Madison slammed down the phone. *Natasha. Oh, Jesus. Stay calm and bloody think.*

She took the lift to the third floor and found Warren Moss's office. "Where's Kimble? I need her now."

Moss looked up from his computer. "On whose authority?"

"I don't have time for this, Warren. Where is she?"

"I sent her to records an hour ago."

Madison ran for the lift and called to Alex Kimble when the doors opened. "Come with me. We need to talk."

Alex obeyed without a word.

They stepped into an empty conference room and Madison closed the door. "I only have enough time to tell you this once, Alex. You've got to remember everything. Understand?"

She began briefing Alex Kimble as quickly as possible. "Now, remember your signals and handle the Russian very carefully. He'll be carrying a diplomatic passport and he won't be in a cooperative mood. You've got to leave now. Time's short."

Alex Kimble looked at her, stunned. "God, Madison, I hope I'm ready for this."

"You'll handle it, Alex, and you'll handle it well."

Madison watched the young agent rush to the elevator, then dialed the Director upstairs. "I need a chopper, sir, and access to the weapons room, and I need it now; I haven't time to explain. You'll have to trust me."

# — 12 —

Alex Kimble took a taxi to Kemp Street, instructing the driver to drop her at the corner, as sound tradecraft demanded. The evening was hazy and damp. The moon would be hidden tonight, she thought as she crossed over wet lawns.

The curtains were pulled open on the front window. The lights, Madison had told her, were never turned on and the curtains never closed until Krasavchenko had arrived for the meetings. It was the signal that told him all was well and there was no surveillance on the street.

She walked around the house and paused by the back door, switching on her penlight twice. Two tiny white flashes answered her signal and let her know the backup team was waiting somewhere in the darkness. Alex would use the same signal once more before the night was over.

She went in through the kitchen door and used the penlight to find her way around, committing to memory the distance from chair to chair, door to door, lest she stumble at some critical moment.

Upstairs, she turned on the voice-activated system and searched for someplace to hide. The bedroom, she thought at first, and then decided it was too distant and too risky. There were creaky floorboards to be considered. Downstairs she found a living room-dining room combination, one closet near the entrance, the kitchen around a corner with swinging saloon doors and a small room with washer and dryer. Deciding at last on the kitchen, she leaned against the far side of the refrigerator and waited.

The house was cold. She waited there with gun in hand, shivering, her eyes moving sharply to the kitchen door with each imagined sound, each passing car, each creak of the old house.

Another car ... Had it passed? Moments later the sound of one pair of feet on the wooden porch. Now the key. Now the door. Now a footfall in the kitchen. Alex's pulse quickened. She saw a light dart across the floor briefly and realized Bradford too had come with a flashlight. She heard him moving around the house and wondered what he was doing, heard the muffled sound of his cough and tried in vain to guess whose cough it might be. It was a deep cough, a smoker's cough. Which one of them smoked? She cursed herself silently for not remembering.

The kitchen doors swung open and Alex stepped around the corner and flattened herself against the wall, her body trembling. The light from his flashlight bobbed across the floor and passed over her feet once. She froze, stopped breathing. Had he seen? No ... The ice box was opening, ice cubes falling into a glass, then another glass. She heard a bottle neck clang against the glasses, heard water running. Bradford was making drinks for himself and his Soviet controller. *You're a good mole, Bradford.*

The front door opened and she heard a smooth, accented voice, heard the curtains closing, and saw the light become suddenly bright as the living room lamps were switched on.

"You do not look good, my friend," said Dmitri Krasavchenko.

Then she heard the muffled reply of a male voice and moved closer to the door.

"You handled it badly with Richard Ward," the Russian continued. "You should have let it happen. We were in no danger."

"I know," was the reply. "But it wasn't working. McGuire fucked up everything. If she'd just brought him in in the beginning everything would have been fine. I didn't know what the hell else to do."

The voice, Kimble thought, I know that voice. Suddenly it hit her full force. It was the voice of the Deputy Director of Operations, her superior, William Ryan.

Alex listened while Ryan told Dmitri of Madison's

160

appearance at Langley today, heard Ryan speak of the Director's suspicions. *And you took the bait, you bastard.*

She moved silently to the kitchen window, cupped her hands around the penlight and pressed the switch twice, then started for the living room. She remembered Madison's warning: Careful with the Russian. Oh so careful, she thought, pushing open the kitchen doors and facing William Ryan and the Soviet Commercial Attache, her 9mm raised, both hands holding it steady.

"*Kimble,*" Ryan declared, and she saw the shock in his eyes. But Will Ryan was an old hand at dealing with surprise and he recovered quickly. "What the hell are you doing here? You don't have clearance for this operation. I'll have you sweeping out the corridors for this."

"It's over, Mr. Ryan. You have no authority here anymore," she said, and saw Ryan close his eyes for just a moment.

Krasavchenko began voicing his objections loudly. "You have no right to detain a Soviet diplomat in this manner." His hand moved towards the inside breast pocket of his jacket. "I have a diplomatic passport and diplomatic — "

Oh so careful . . . "Keep that hand where I can see it, Mr. Krasavchenko," Alex ordered, trying to keep the shake from her voice.

John Crawford and his backup team burst through the door. Alex heard Crawford's hurried orders to his team through the ringing in her ears. The Director was on his way, Crawford told her, as his group spread out through the house. All the lights were turned on. Doors swung open, rooms were searched. There was banging and heavy footsteps upstairs. There was William Ryan, traitor, standing quietly, detached, looking at no one. Then the brisk arrival of the Director who barely looked at Ryan before barking orders for Crawford and his team to wait outside and leading Krasavchenko into the kitchen.

Finally there was only Ryan who had been searched and was now sitting on the sofa, legs crossed, hands folded tidily over his knees.

He watched Alex calmly as Mitchell Colby and Dmitri Krasavchenko disappeared into the kitchen. "Do you know what's going on now, Kimble? They're working out a deal, deciding what to do with me. I imagine Mitchell will decide it's best for the agency if they pack me off quietly to Moscow."

He had said it as if it were someone else's story, as if he had heard it second-hand. His voice was removed from the context of his words, unconcerned.

"I don't care what they do with you," Alex answered, knowing Ryan's astonishing indifference and her own sense of sudden anticlimax had added a strange unreality to the evening.

Ryan smiled, but there was no humor in his eyes. "I suppose you see exile as an easy way out for someone like me. It's all politics, Kimble. You'll learn the game."

The Director stepped out of the kitchen with Dmitri Krasavchenko. He glanced at Ryan and opened the front door, snarling orders to Crawford, "Get the tapes and get him out of my sight."

Dmitri sat down next to Ryan. "I've agreed to no publicity on the condition that they release you to us in a few days. Are you going to be all right? Is there anything you need?"

Ryan shook his head and John Crawford took his arm.

Alex Kimble watched Ryan being escorted to a waiting van, watched his back as he walked away without a struggle. She turned to the Director who had been watching too. He had the bewildered look of a father who had been betrayed. He wrapped an arm around her shoulders briefly, then without a word walked away from her and out of the safe house.


Once the chopper was in the air, she slipped into her night-time clothes and checked her supplies: a double-sided knife, a spool of thin wire, a ski mask, a roll of wide tape, a pair of Zeiss night vision binoculars, a silencer. She checked her weapon, a 9mm Sig Sauer, and dropped two full magazines into her pocket.

The chopper hovered over an empty strip of beach approximately two miles from the house. Natasha Vladov would not be alerted to her arrival. Surprise was vital.

The sky was moonless. The unlit night was a friend. She did not fear the darkness, she embraced it gratefully. It had cloaked her in the past as she moved towards enemy camps, taut, alert to any movement, trained for infiltration.

The Scorpion, the code name Madison had been given years ago on a warm, dark Venezuelan night, was coming alive in her again. The code name she had earned that night when a band of extremists had held the Ambassador and three agents of the CIA hostage. The Scorpion, the creature that suddenly moves in on its victim and terminates silently with a venomous sting, had been born on that black night. And tonight, as she slipped the ski mask over her head and trotted noiselessly down the beach, she welcomed back that part of herself. Her mind focused on one thing only: freeing Terry at any price.

From her spot on the beach, the house looked like a great, huge, shadowy box, sitting alone above the water without a neighbor within a half mile, one dim light glowing in the living room.

How many patrols were waiting? How many nameless faces between her and Terry?

Then, a light in the darkness ... A match, a brief white flash in a cupped hand. Was it Vladov? No. Vladov was too smart for such a mistake. An impatient guard who could not wait for a cigarette.

Madison withdrew the binoculars and through the infrared lenses saw a man standing alone on the beach yards below the deck. Keeping low to the ground, she headed for the side of the house and saw the outline of another guard standing on the gravel covered drive near the road. *That's two.*

... Voices, low, hushed. Madison crept along the wall of the house and ducked beside Terry's car, scanning the darkness. Two more figures came into view, submachine guns held at their sides. They were talking softly, standing back to back, one watching the beach, the other the road.

Four in all, and one more in the house with Terry. Her surveillance complete, she moved back around the house and leaned against the wall, collecting her thoughts, planning the next move.

Moving cautiously, she stepped below the deck overhang and saw the first guard crushing his cigarette into the sand, his back to her. She took one step forward.

The ground between them suddenly sprang to bright life. The vertical blinds had been pulled back and the sliding glass doors on the deck opened, sending a wash of yellow light over a section of beach. The guard spun around. Madison hit the ground and rolled over, seeing a figure moving over the deck between the cracks in the wood.

A woman's voice . . . "She will not come by boat, Comrade. Watch the beach." The door closed and the light disappeared.

The guard, alert after the reprimand, held his weapon ready to fire and began patrolling the beach. Madison waited for him to start in the other direction before springing to her feet.

In a second she was behind him. "If you move or speak, I'll kill you. Understand, Comrade? Now drop the gun."

He let the weapon fall in the sand then spun around, one leg aimed at her. Madison ducked and came up with her hand held flat, fingers rigid. She directed the blow at his throat, crushing the windpipe instantly.

Three more and one inside, she thought savagely, picking up his weapon and running back to the cover of the house, slowly working her way around to the second patrol.

They had split up and Madison could see only one, leaning against Terry's car, looking into the darkness. She crouched next to the car feeling the perspiration in her palm where she gripped the 9mm. She raised up suddenly and brought the handle of the gun down against the back of his neck. He slid to the ground, limp. Madison tied his wrists and ankles with the wire and ran tape over his mouth. *Two more and one inside.*

She moved down the drive, scanning the area with the night vision binoculars, focusing on a guard near the road. She found a place on the driveway and lay on her stomach, lowering the binoculars and raising the 9mm, but he melted into the darkness once again. *Move this way you bastard and let me have you.*

A car passed on Highway 12. A brief, bright light swept over both Madison and the guard. Raising the 9mm, she fired two shots and grabbed the binoculars. He was lying face down on the driveway.

Then a sound . . . A footstep on the gravel drive. Madison saw him running towards her. Then the loud, hollow burst of his gun . . . Then the quiet spit of Madison's 9mm. Then blackness.

She sat up. How long had she been lying there? Seconds? Hours? Her ribs felt like they were going to explode. She ran her hand along her side and felt the wetness, realizing in one terrifying second that she had been hit.

"Terry," she murmured, pulling off the ski mask, looking towards the house.

The living room light had been extinguished. *Natasha's waiting.*

The walk seemed to go on for miles. The house loomed before her, menacing and dark, cloaked by the fog that had seized her, that had taken control of her eyes, her balance, her judgment. Every step was a near stumble. Every uneven piece of ground, every hole, every mound was a challenge. She likened the sounds to that of putting her ear to a sea shell — a quiet rumble, a vague roar.

Thoughts ran through her mind. There was the practical — slowing her heart rate to slow the bleeding, holding onto the gun, staying near the ground. Then there was the strange, fleeting perception that she might not live, that Terry might die as Elicia had died years ago in London, simply because Madison had loved her.

The front steps were near. Five of them, she knew. She clutched the railing, felt the wood, felt its roughness, grateful for some little piece of reality.

... A quiet turn of the knob, now a step inside, now the light.

They were in the center of the room, Terry tied and gagged in a chair, Natasha concealed behind her body, a pistol at Terry's temple.

Madison raised the 9mm and held it there. "It's over. Bradford's blown by now. It's for nothing, Natasha. Let her go." Her own voice sounded strange and hollow, as if someone else had uttered those words.

A slow, even smile came over Natasha Vladov's face. She saw Madison's drained face, saw the blood collecting at Madison's feet. "That is the difference between us," Natasha said. "For you it is ideology. For me it is business. It will be an impressive addition to my resume, killing the acclaimed Scorpion."

Madison tightened her grip on the Sig Sauer and

blinked away the mist that was forming over her eyes.

"Ah." Natasha seemed amused. "Perhaps we are not so different. Your finger tightens on the trigger. You would gamble with your lover's life. Are you strong enough? Are you still quick enough for such a costly wager?"

Madison's face felt hot. Her eyes felt dry, and it crossed her mind that Natasha's voice sounded very distant and artificial. She looked at Terry and saw tears streaking her face, saw the scared, wide eyes, and for one startling moment Madison McGuire was more lucid than she had ever been in her life. She was looking down the barrel of the 9mm, and there she saw the dark eyes of her enemy. They were not the obsessed eyes of a fanatic, not the darting, angry eyes of a terrorist. They were the eyes of a killer who was cold and calm and superior in her ability to kill dispassionately.

The eyes blinked ... Madison fired ...

She saw Natasha's head jerk backwards, its top blown off, saw the gun drop from Natasha's hand and she started for Terry, unsteadily at first, then finding life in her legs. Terry's eyes widened in horror when Madison reached around to remove the gag ... And then Madison saw it under the chair — a digital clock face, ticking off the seconds. It was attached to a tin box, a miniature claymore mine, fused electronically, improvised and crude, but effective nonetheless. One minute thirty seconds remained on the counter. Natasha must have activated the timer when she heard the gunshots outside.

"I'm going to untie you, darling," she told Terry.

"But you mustn't move." The tears were still coming and Terry took an enormous breath of air when the gag came off.

Madison knelt beside the chair and studied the bomb carefully. Two leg wires ran to the timer. One was a decoy, one would activate the detonator.

She ran her hands along the base of the box, and through the dreamlike unreality that had seized her once again, she realized that her fingers were oily, and that Natasha Vladov had made an error. She had cut the hole in the base of the box a hair too large and had used petroleum jelly as a filler to hold the blasting cap.

"I think I've got it," she said weakly, and checked the timer ... Twenty seconds.

She placed her thumb and forefinger around the blasting cap and tugged gently. She heard it pop, felt the burn in her palm as it passed by her hand and onto the floor. She was losing control now, felt herself drifting, and then she had the vague perception of falling backwards, of seeing the overhead light, clouded and smoky. She saw movement, a figure moving to loom over her. She heard a voice but could not grasp its meaning.

# Epilogue

The hollow bell rang four times at the top of each hour. It had done this as long as she could remember, and no one in the town of Whitby seemed inclined to repair the graceless old clock in the tower that rose above two-story homes with flagstone walks and fences with gates that hadn't been mended for years. Beneath the tower, an empty bandstand stood alone in the center of the Square, its white paint flaking from the constant battering of salt air. She had sat on that bandstand once years ago, her legs dangling off the edge. It had comforted her then, and it conforted her now, knowing her father had been there, knowing her father had loved Whitby as she loved it now, loved its quiet, loved its winds and its salt air.

She had come here three days after the messenger had delivered the news, wanting to feel the peace her father had felt here, wanting to remember him in his quiet moments, needing the undisturbed calm he had once drawn from this place. He had come here after the death of her mother, come here with her ashes and watched the wind and the water take them out to sea, as she had come with his many years later. Whitby was a place of goodbyes, of quiet farewells.

She walked, with her suitcase and two packages under her arm, past the bus station and a small market, past doorways and porches with rocking chairs, past front windows with curtains that parted at the sound of an engine.

She opened the gate carefully and propped it back on the stone that raised it to the height of the latch, making a mental note to buy an extra hinge.

Mrs. Bishop's long face peered out suspiciously at the metallic sound of the gate squeaking open. A widow can't be too careful these days, Mrs. Bishop had once told her.

"Ms. Waterford," the old woman said, opening the door for Madison. "Come in, then. You'll catch your death out there." She hurried Madison into the boarding house and shut the door. "What's kept you so long then? Barely a card in over a year," she objected, in the voice of a mother who had been forgotten on the holidays. "It's your articles, is it? That's what kept you away. Been selling a lot to the

**171**

magazines, have you? You look so thin. Sit down. I'll get your biscuits and tea."

Madison pulled the boxes from under her arm, one neatly wrapped. "I've something for you, Mrs. Bishop, and Clancy too."

Mrs. Bishop started complaining right off, scolding Madison for her extravagance, and Madison smiled, knowing full well that her surprises were something Mrs. Bishop always looked forward to.

"Clancy," she called out, "here then, boy. Ms. Waterford has come to see us." She confided solemnly, "He's half deaf these days, you know. Clancy, come *here*."

A shaggy brown mutt rounded the corner, one ear turned inside out, tail wagging expectantly. "Ms. Waterford has something for you. A little snack. Go on then, take it."

Clancy took a dog biscuit from Mrs. Bishop's hand and carried it protectively into the kitchen.

"It's your turn," Madison said, and Mrs. Bishop took the box, carefully peeling away the paper as if she might want to use it again. It was a long flannel dressing gown, the kind Mrs. Bishop told Madison she had always wanted to keep her warm at night. She stepped in front of the hall mirror and held it to her crooked little body approvingly.

They had tea and biscuits in the sitting room downstairs. Its walls were covered with little pink roses on paper yellowed with age, and the end tables showed off pictures from Mrs. Bishop's past. Her life till now, as far as Madison could tell, had been a catalog of grand and heroic deaths. Her father and two brothers had died fighting wars, her mother had died fighting her father long before, and her husband had died fighting cancer. They had each left a bit of themselves behind for her, a small inheritance — the house she lived in, the garden she worked in, a sharp, alert mind, and a fiercely independent soul.

Madison inquired about her garden, knowing it was the only thing Mrs. Bishop loved as much as Clancy. She asked to be caught up on the local gossip and listened intently to news that held little interest for her except in hearing Mrs. Bishop's wonderful, crackling voice listing her complaints one by one about the state of the country, about boarders who had come and gone leaving her rooms in a dreadful state, about Clancy's encounter with a larger dog and his emergency visit to the veterinarian, about Mr. Poole across the Square who had disappeared for a month and come back with a young man he claimed was his live-in gardener.

And when Madison finished her tea and tried to hide a yawn, Mrs. Bishop insisted she go to her room for a nice nap before the evening meal.

"I'll be staying awhile this time. I hope it's all right."

Mrs. Bishop waved her away. "Go on, then. Have your nap."

Approvingly, she watched Madison climb the stairs, suitcase in hand. It would be nice to have Ms. Waterford back again, she told Clancy in the kitchen. This tenant had always been one of the good ones. Quiet and clean, always willing to help out when things got too busy, and handy enough, for a woman that is, able even to fix the plumbing when it went down. Why once Ms. Waterford, if that was really her name, for Mrs. Bishop had searched the magazines for articles written under that name and found nothing, had even put a fresh coat of paint on the shutters. And she always paid in advance. Once a year like clockwork Mrs. Bishop received a cashier's check for the upstairs room, the one that looked out over the sea.

Mrs. Bishop wondered what had brought her back this time, wondered whatever had brought her to a tiny coastal town in the first place. She had come at all hours over the years, arriving in the middle of a rainy night or early in the morning, apologizing quietly for the disturbance. She had come in the afternoons and in the evenings, and on Mrs. Bishop's birthday she had come early with a handsome bakery-made cake. She had said she needed the time away to write her articles. She had offered nothing about her life away from Whitby, never given an opinon when Mrs. Bishop had tried to draw her into a political discussion, never spoke of love or family.

"She's a spy, Clancy, that's what, and all alone in the world, is my bet. We're all she's got and we mustn't trouble her with our questions."

Madison tossed her suitcase on the bed and lit a cigarette, knowing Mrs. Bishop always pretended to be furious with her for smoking in the house, and knowing too that Mrs. Bishop needed something to be furious about. She opened the dressing table drawer, found the ashtray Mrs. Bishop put there for her, and slipped off her sweater, loosening the bandage around the rib that had been cracked, the rib that had saved her life by deflecting a bullet just enough on a dark Carolina night.

She crossed to the window. The sky was white behind the glass and the waves were breaking high and hard against the rocks. She thought of Ryan and searched for some explanation that would satisfy her hunger to understand his motives, remembering their last conversation.

Ryan had asked for her on his last day in America and she had gone to the Virginia farm where he was being held by the interrogators. He was lying on a bunk bed, ankles crossed, hands behind his head.

"Ah," he said smiling. "Here she comes. A singular spy if ever there was one."

"This started in Czechoslovakia, didn't it, Will? Twenty years ago you made a deal to get those two American agents out after the Prague revolution. Why didn't you tell someone? The Company would have understood. We could have used you as a double. You didn't have to go this far."

Ryan laughed. "And now the triumphant agent wants the heart-wrenching explanation. Let's see." He sat up and put one finger to his chin — a man deep in thought. "How about, I wasn't loved as a child? Or maybe you're looking for one event that converted me. Cuba? Vietnam? Cambodia? What would make you feel better about your victory, Madison?" He shrugged. "What can I say? I liked the structure of it all."

Madison studied him carefully for a moment. "That's a very neat explanation from a man who would sell himself to save his agents."

He seemed to drift away for a moment. "In the early days they came pretty often," he said quietly. "Some women, some men, but they always used the same code name. It was Bradford. They thought it was a good American name. God, I used to dread their visits. I hated them at first, hated what they had turned me into, hated them squeezing little bits of information out of me. And they wanted everything. Details, gossip, anything I'd give them. And then, Madison, a strange thing happened. It was in the second year, I think, weeks, sometimes months would pass without a contact. I started to miss them in a strange way. The longer they stayed away the more inadequate I felt. I found myself worrying about whether I'd given them what they wanted, worried that they no longer valued me. God, they were smart, taking a little here and a little there, then leaving me like an abandoned child. You see, they knew I'd come to need them, knew they were the only ones in the whole goddamned world who knew what I really was. You need that after a while. It's how they hook you. It's how you end up loving them more." He paused and thought for a moment. "I'm a hero over there, you know."

Madison had leaned back against the wall that day and closed her eyes. Some little part of her, she supposed, had suspected Ryan all along. Ryan and his boyish good looks. Ryan and his outstanding career. Perhaps Mitchell Colby had had the same unspoken suspicious.

It all made perfect sense now. The Kemp Street house had been reserved for the meetings between Krasavchenko and Ryan, giving Ryan access to his Soviet controller anytime without question, while the

Russian posed as a double agent, passing Langley only enough information to keep them believing the myth. It was brilliant, a perfect cover.

And then she thought of Dan Wright, blown in Moscow for entertainment's sake, coming back in God only knew what kind of condition. She thought of Frank Blitzer, who had loved Ryan, and who now limped into a dull insurance office every day. She thought of Donna Sykes, watching over her dogs and making up stories about the glory days. As she thought of Charlie and the Russian scientist and all the other casualties of Witness, of Night Trace, of Bradford, a wave of anger swept over her. He had betrayed them all — his colleagues, his friends, his family, his country — and Madison knew that even now she could not fully grasp the magnitude of his deception.

"You were a hero here, Will," she had said bitterly. "To people like Frank Blitzer, who adored you and took bullets for you."

Ryan looked at her strangely. "Who?"

"Why did you want to see me?" Madison asked quietly.

William Ryan let out an enormous sigh. "Will you see my wife, break it to her gently? It's going to be a shock. She didn't know." He thought for a moment. "It wasn't personal, you know. I lost control over Natasha. She wanted you from the beginning. I'm sorry you were hurt. I really am. And your friend in Lucerne. What was his name?"

"Charlie," Madison had told him. Then turned her back on him and walked out.

It had appealed to his sense of order, he had said. Could treason ever be so simple? Had he betrayed his country simply because he liked the "structure" of elitist rule?

She remembered the wife he left behind and she puzzled over the concern he displayed for her even while he prepared for his defection to the Soviet Union. Remembered her stunned expression as Madison tried to find a way to tell her that her husband had been a traitor. Remembered the denial in her eyes, the hands that grasped the back of a chair for support.

William Ryan was a man of contrasts, a man who must have enjoyed playing world against world, agent against agent, a man who had needed so much, a man wooed by the idea of being a hero in an aristocracy he had not been born into. William Ryan must have been a very sad man, she decided.

Her eyes wandered over the boarding house room. A picture of a lighthouse hung over the bed. She thought of Terry then, of the pictures they had hung together, of Christmas presents she never got around to buying for Terry.

She remembered leaving, remembered her own words: "You deserve more than being left alone night after night, you deserve a normal life without the stress of worrying about me and you certainly deserve a relationship that isn't actually physically threatening to you."

And Terry's response had been so simple, so uncomplicated — a decision that would have been so easy for Terry herself: "All you have to do is walk away from the agency, Madison. That's all."

And then Terry's words as she drove away. "Leave me for something I can understand," she had shouted through her tears. "Something real. Another woman, another life. But don't leave me for the Company! Don't make some private sacrifice for me, you don't have the right!"

But Madison had had to leave. Her secret world had seeped into their home, had very nearly killed Terry.

She remembered seeing the Christmas tree in the corner of the living room as she had taken a last look at what she was leaving, remembered Stray Cat lying on the couch, indifferent, remembered the betrayed look in Terry's dark eyes.

God, she would miss those eyes.

She took a picture of Terry from her bag and held it in her hands for a while, then turned back to the sea.

A few of the publications of
**THE NAIAD PRESS, INC.**
P.O. Box 10543 • Tallahassee, Florida 32302
Phone (904) 539-5965
*Mail orders welcome. Please include 15% postage.*

A SINGULAR SPY by Amanda K. Williams. 192 pp. Third spy novel
featuring Lesbian agent Madison McGuire.     ISBN 1-56280-008-6     $8.95

THE END OF APRIL by Penny Sumner. 240 pp. A Victoria Cross
Mystery. First in a series.     ISBN 1-56280-007-8     8.95

A FLIGHT OF ANGELS by Sarah Aldridge. 240 pp. Romance set at
the National Gallery of Art     ISBN 1-56280-001-9     9.95

HOUSTON TOWN by Deborah Powell. 208 pp. A Hollis Carpenter
mystery. Second in a series.     ISBN 1-56280-006-X     8.95

KISS AND TELL by Robbi Sommers. 192 pp. Scorching stories by
the author of *Pleasures*.     ISBN 1-56280-005-1     8.95

STILL WATERS by Pat Welch. 208 pp. Second in the Helen
Black mystery series.     ISBN 0-941483-97-5     8.95

MURDER IS GERMANE by Karen Saum. 224 pp. The 2nd
Brigid Donovan mystery.     ISBN 0-941483-98-3     8.95

TO LOVE AGAIN by Evelyn Kennedy. 208 pp. Wildly
romantic love story.     ISBN 0-941483-85-1     9.95

IN THE GAME by Nikki Baker. 192 pp. A Virginia Kelly
mystery. First in a series.     ISBN 01-56280-004-3     8.95

AVALON by Mary Jane Jones. 256 pp. A Lesbian Arthurian
romance.     ISBN 0-941483-96-7     9.95

STRANDED by Camarin Grae. 320 pp. Entertaining, riveting
adventure.     ISBN 0-941483-99-1     9.95

THE DAUGHTERS OF ARTEMIS by Lauren Wright Douglas.
240 pp. Third Caitlin Reece mystery.     ISBN 0-941483-95-9     8.95

CLEARWATER by Catherine Ennis. 176 pp. Romantic secrets
of a small Louisiana town.     ISBN 0-941483-65-7     8.95

THE HALLELUJAH MURDERS by Dorothy Tell. 176 pp.
Second Poppy Dillworth mystery.     ISBN 0-941483-88-6     8.95

ZETA BASE by Judith Alguire. 208 pp. Lesbian triangle
on a future Earth.     ISBN 0-941483-94-0     9.95

SECOND CHANCE by Jackie Calhoun. 256 pp. Contemporary
Lesbian lives and loves.     ISBN 0-941483-93-2     9.95

MURDER BY TRADITION by Katherine V. Forrest. 288 pp.
A Kate Delafield Mystery. 4th in a series.     ISBN 0-941483-89-4     18.95

BENEDICTION by Diane Salvatore. 272 pp. Striking,
contemporary romantic novel.               ISBN 0-941483-90-8     9.95

CALLING RAIN by Karen Marie Christa Minns. 240 pp.
Spellbinding, erotic love story            ISBN 0-941483-87-8     9.95

BLACK IRIS by Jeane Harris. 192 pp. Caroline's hidden past . . .
                                           ISBN 0-941483-68-1     8.95

TOUCHWOOD by Karin Kallmaker. 240 pp. Loving, May/
December romance.                          ISBN 0-941483-76-2     8.95

BAYOU CITY SECRETS by Deborah Powell. 224 pp. A Hollis
Carpenter mystery. First in a series.      ISBN 0-941483-91-6     8.95

COP OUT by Claire McNab. 208 pp. 4th Det. Insp. Carol Ashton
mystery.                                   ISBN 0-941483-84-3     8.95

LODESTAR by Phyllis Horn. 224 pp. Romantic, fast-moving
adventure.                                 ISBN 0-941483-83-5     8.95

THE BEVERLY MALIBU by Katherine V. Forrest. 288 pp. A
Kate Delafield Mystery. 3rd in a series. (HC)  ISBN 0-941483-47-9  16.95
                         Paperback   ISBN 0-941483-48-7     9.95

THAT OLD STUDEBAKER by Lee Lynch. 272 pp. Andy's affair
with Regina and her attachment to her beloved car.
                                           ISBN 0-941483-82-7     9.95

PASSION'S LEGACY by Lori Paige. 224 pp. Sarah is swept into
the arms of Augusta Pym in this delightful historical romance.
                                           ISBN 0-941483-81-9     8.95

THE PROVIDENCE FILE by Amanda Kyle Williams. 256 pp.
Second espionage thriller featuring lesbian agent Madison McGuire
                                           ISBN 0-941483-92-4     8.95

I LEFT MY HEART by Jaye Maiman. 320 pp. A Robin Miller
Mystery. First in a series.                ISBN 0-941483-72-X     9.95

THE PRICE OF SALT by Patricia Highsmith (writing as Claire
Morgan). 288 pp. Classic lesbian novel, first issued in 1952 . . .
acknowledged by its author under her own, very famous, name.
                                           ISBN 1-56280-003-5     8.95

SIDE BY SIDE by Isabel Miller. 256 pp. From beloved author of
*Patience and Sarah*.                      ISBN 0-941483-77-0     8.95

SOUTHBOUND by Sheila Ortiz Taylor. 240 pp. Hilarious sequel
to *Faultline*.                            ISBN 0-941483-78-9     8.95

STAYING POWER: LONG TERM LESBIAN COUPLES
by Susan E. Johnson. 352 pp. Joys of coupledom.
                                           ISBN 0-941-483-75-4   12.95

SLICK by Camarin Grae. 304 pp. Exotic, erotic adventure.
                                           ISBN 0-941483-74-6     9.95

NINTH LIFE by Lauren Wright Douglas. 256 pp. A Caitlin
Reece mystery. 2nd in a series.            ISBN 0-941483-50-9     8.95

LIFTING BELLY by Gertrude Stein. Ed. by Rebecca Mark. 104
pp. Erotic poetry. ISBN 0-941483-51-7 8.95
ISBN 0-941483-53-3 14.95

ROSE PENSKI by Roz Perry. 192 pp. Adult lovers in a long-term
relationship. ISBN 0-941483-37-1 8.95

AFTER THE FIRE by Jane Rule. 256 pp. Warm, human novel
by this incomparable author. ISBN 0-941483-45-2 8.95

SUE SLATE, PRIVATE EYE by Lee Lynch. 176 pp. The gay
folk of Peacock Alley are *all cats.* ISBN 0-941483-52-5 8.95

CHRIS by Randy Salem. 224 pp. Golden oldie. Handsome Chris
and her adventures. ISBN 0-941483-42-8 8.95

THREE WOMEN by March Hastings. 232 pp. Golden oldie. A
triangle among wealthy sophisticates. ISBN 0-941483-43-6 8.95

RICE AND BEANS by Valeria Taylor. 232 pp. Love and
romance on poverty row. ISBN 0-941483-41-X 8.95

PLEASURES by Robbi Sommers. 204 pp. Unprecedented
eroticism. ISBN 0-941483-49-5 8.95

EDGEWISE by Camarin Grae. 372 pp. Spellbinding
adventure. ISBN 0-941483-19-3 9.95

FATAL REUNION by Claire McNab. 224 pp. 2nd Det. Inspec.
Carol Ashton mystery. ISBN 0-941483-40-1 8.95

KEEP TO ME STRANGER by Sarah Aldridge. 372 pp. Romance
set in a department store dynasty. ISBN 0-941483-38-X 9.95

HEARTSCAPE by Sue Gambill. 204 pp. American lesbian in
Portugal. ISBN 0-941483-33-9 8.95

IN THE BLOOD by Lauren Wright Douglas. 252 pp. Lesbian
science fiction adventure fantasy ISBN 0-941483-22-3 8.95

THE BEE'S KISS by Shirley Verel. 216 pp. Delicate, delicious
romance. ISBN 0-941483-36-3 8.95

RAGING MOTHER MOUNTAIN by Pat Emmerson. 264 pp.
Furosa Firechild's adventures in Wonderland. ISBN 0-941483-35-5 8.95

IN EVERY PORT by Karin Kallmaker. 228 pp. Jessica's sexy,
adventuresome travels. ISBN 0-941483-37-7 8.95

OF LOVE AND GLORY by Evelyn Kennedy. 192 pp. Exciting
WWII romance. ISBN 0-941483-32-0 8.95

CLICKING STONES by Nancy Tyler Glenn. 288 pp. Love
transcending time. ISBN 0-941483-31-2 9.95

SURVIVING SISTERS by Gail Pass. 252 pp. Powerful love
story. ISBN 0-941483-16-9 8.95

SOUTH OF THE LINE by Catherine Ennis. 216 pp. Civil War
adventure. ISBN 0-941483-29-0 8.95

WOMAN PLUS WOMAN by Dolores Klaich. 300 pp. Supurb
Lesbian overview.                                 ISBN 0-941483-28-2   9.95

SLOW DANCING AT MISS POLLY'S by Sheila Ortiz Taylor.
96 pp. Lesbian Poetry                             ISBN 0-941483-30-4   7.95

DOUBLE DAUGHTER by Vicki P. McConnell. 216 pp. A Nyla
Wade Mystery, third in the series.                ISBN 0-941483-26-6   8.95

HEAVY GILT by Delores Klaich. 192 pp. Lesbian detective/
disappearing homophobes/upper class gay society.
                                                  ISBN 0-941483-25-8   8.95

THE FINER GRAIN by Denise Ohio. 216 pp. Brilliant young
college lesbian novel.                            ISBN 0-941483-11-8   8.95

THE AMAZON TRAIL by Lee Lynch. 216 pp. Life, travel & lore
of famous lesbian author.                         ISBN 0-941483-27-4   8.95

HIGH CONTRAST by Jessie Lattimore. 264 pp. Women of the
Crystal Palace.                                   ISBN 0-941483-17-7   8.95

OCTOBER OBSESSION by Meredith More. Josie's rich, secret
Lesbian life.                                     ISBN 0-941483-18-5   8.95

LESBIAN CROSSROADS by Ruth Baetz. 276 pp. Contemporary
Lesbian lives.                                    ISBN 0-941483-21-5   9.95

BEFORE STONEWALL: THE MAKING OF A GAY AND
LESBIAN COMMUNITY by Andrea Weiss & Greta Schiller.
96 pp., 25 illus.                                 ISBN 0-941483-20-7   7.95

WE WALK THE BACK OF THE TIGER by Patricia A. Murphy.
192 pp. Romantic Lesbian novel/beginning women's movement.
                                                  ISBN 0-941483-13-4   8.95

SUNDAY'S CHILD by Joyce Bright. 216 pp. Lesbian athletics, at
last the novel about sports.                      ISBN 0-941483-12-6   8.95

OSTEN'S BAY by Zenobia N. Vole. 204 pp. Sizzling adventure
romance set on Bonaire.                           ISBN 0-941483-15-0   8.95

LESSONS IN MURDER by Claire McNab. 216 pp. 1st Det. Inspec.
Carol Ashton mystery — erotic tension!.           ISBN 0-941483-14-2   8.95

YELLOWTHROAT by Penny Hayes. 240 pp. Margarita, bandit,
kidnaps Julia.                                    ISBN 0-941483-10-X   8.95

SAPPHISTRY: THE BOOK OF LESBIAN SEXUALITY by
Pat Califia. 3d edition, revised. 208 pp.         ISBN 0-941483-24-X   8.95

CHERISHED LOVE by Evelyn Kennedy. 192 pp. Erotic
Lesbian love story.                               ISBN 0-941483-08-8   8.95

LAST SEPTEMBER by Helen R. Hull. 208 pp. Six stories & a
glorious novella.                                 ISBN 0-941483-09-6   8.95

THE SECRET IN THE BIRD by Camarin Grae. 312 pp. Striking,
psychological suspense novel.                     ISBN 0-941483-05-3   8.95

TO THE LIGHTNING by Catherine Ennis. 208 pp. Romantic
Lesbian 'Robinson Crusoe' adventure.  ISBN 0-941483-06-1  8.95

THE OTHER SIDE OF VENUS by Shirley Verel. 224 pp.
Luminous, romantic love story.  ISBN 0-941483-07-X  8.95

DREAMS AND SWORDS by Katherine V. Forrest. 192 pp.
Romantic, erotic, imaginative stories.  ISBN 0-941483-03-7  8.95

MEMORY BOARD by Jane Rule. 336 pp. Memorable novel
about an aging Lesbian couple.  ISBN 0-941483-02-9  9.95

THE ALWAYS ANONYMOUS BEAST by Lauren Wright
Douglas. 224 pp. A Caitlin Reece mystery. First in a series.
ISBN 0-941483-04-5  8.95

SEARCHING FOR SPRING by Patricia A. Murphy. 224 pp.
Novel about the recovery of love.  ISBN 0-941483-00-2  8.95

DUSTY'S QUEEN OF HEARTS DINER by Lee Lynch. 240 pp.
Romantic blue-collar novel.  ISBN 0-941483-01-0  8.95

PARENTS MATTER by Ann Muller. 240 pp. Parents'
relationships with Lesbian daughters and gay sons.
ISBN 0-930044-91-6  9.95

THE PEARLS by Shelley Smith. 176 pp. Passion and fun in
the Caribbean sun.  ISBN 0-930044-93-2  7.95

MAGDALENA by Sarah Aldridge. 352 pp. Epic Lesbian novel
set on three continents.  ISBN 0-930044-99-1  8.95

THE BLACK AND WHITE OF IT by Ann Allen Shockley.
144 pp. Short stories.  ISBN 0-930044-96-7  7.95

SAY JESUS AND COME TO ME by Ann Allen Shockley. 288
pp. Contemporary romance.  ISBN 0-930044-98-3  8.95

LOVING HER by Ann Allen Shockley. 192 pp. Romantic love
story.  ISBN 0-930044-97-5  7.95

MURDER AT THE NIGHTWOOD BAR by Katherine V.
Forrest. 240 pp. A Kate Delafield mystery. Second in a series.
ISBN 0-930044-92-4  9.95

ZOE'S BOOK by Gail Pass. 224 pp. Passionate, obsessive love
story.  ISBN 0-930044-95-9  7.95

WINGED DANCER by Camarin Grae. 228 pp. Erotic Lesbian
adventure story.  ISBN 0-930044-88-6  8.95

PAZ by Camarin Grae. 336 pp. Romantic Lesbian adventurer
with the power to change the world.  ISBN 0-930044-89-4  8.95

SOUL SNATCHER by Camarin Grae. 224 pp. A puzzle, an
adventure, a mystery — Lesbian romance.  ISBN 0-930044-90-8  8.95

THE LOVE OF GOOD WOMEN by Isabel Miller. 224 pp.
Long-awaited new novel by the author of the beloved *Patience
and Sarah*.  ISBN 0-930044-81-9  8.95

THE HOUSE AT PELHAM FALLS by Brenda Weathers. 240
pp. Suspenseful Lesbian ghost story.          ISBN 0-930044-79-7      7.95

HOME IN YOUR HANDS by Lee Lynch. 240 pp. More stories
from the author of *Old Dyke Tales.*          ISBN 0-930044-80-0      7.95

EACH HAND A MAP by Anita Skeen. 112 pp. Real-life poems
that touch us all.                            ISBN 0-930044-82-7      6.95

SURPLUS by Sylvia Stevenson. 342 pp. A classic early Lesbian
novel.                                        ISBN 0-930044-78-9      7.95

PEMBROKE PARK by Michelle Martin. 256 pp. Derring-do
and daring romance in Regency England.        ISBN 0-930044-77-0      7.95

THE LONG TRAIL by Penny Hayes. 248 pp. Vivid adventures
of two women in love in the old west.         ISBN 0-930044-76-2      8.95

HORIZON OF THE HEART by Shelley Smith. 192 pp. Hot
romance in summertime New England.            ISBN 0-930044-75-4      7.95

AN EMERGENCE OF GREEN by Katherine V. Forrest. 288
pp. Powerful novel of sexual discovery.       ISBN 0-930044-69-X      9.95

THE LESBIAN PERIODICALS INDEX edited by Claire
Potter. 432 pp. Author & subject index.       ISBN 0-930044-74-6     29.95

DESERT OF THE HEART by Jane Rule. 224 pp. A classic;
basis for the movie *Desert Hearts.*          ISBN 0-930044-73-8      8.95

SPRING FORWARD/FALL BACK by Sheila Ortiz Taylor.
288 pp. Literary novel of timeless love.      ISBN 0-930044-70-3      7.95

FOR KEEPS by Elisabeth Nonas. 144 pp. Contemporary novel
about losing and finding love.                ISBN 0-930044-71-1      7.95

TORCHLIGHT TO VALHALLA by Gale Wilhelm. 128 pp.
Classic novel by a great Lesbian writer.      ISBN 0-930044-68-1      7.95

LESBIAN NUNS: BREAKING SILENCE edited by Rosemary
Curb and Nancy Manahan. 432 pp. Unprecedented autobiographies
of religious life.                            ISBN 0-930044-62-2      9.95

THE SWASHBUCKLER by Lee Lynch. 288 pp. Colorful novel
set in Greenwich Village in the sixties.      ISBN 0-930044-66-5      8.95

MISFORTUNE'S FRIEND by Sarah Aldridge. 320 pp. Histori-
cal Lesbian novel set on two continents.      ISBN 0-930044-67-3      7.95

A STUDIO OF ONE'S OWN by Ann Stokes. Edited by
Dolores Klaich. 128 pp. Autobiography.        ISBN 0-930044-64-9      7.95


These are just a few of the many Naiad Press titles — we are the oldest and
largest lesbian/feminist publishing company in the world. Please request a
complete catalog. We offer personal service; we encourage and welcome direct
mail orders from individuals who have limited access to bookstores carrying
our publications.